ALSO AVAILABLE

STAR SWITCH

ALESHA DIXON

IN COLLABORATION WITH

KATY BIRCHALL

M SCHOLASTIC

Published in the UK by Scholastic Children's Books, 2020
Euston House, 24 Eversholt Street, London, NW1 1DB, UK
A division of Scholastic Limited.

London – New York – Toronto – Sydney – Auckland
Mexico City – New Delhi – Hong Kong

Text © Alesha Dixon, 2020
Front cover character art by Nuno Ramalhão © Scholastic, 2020

The right of Alesha Dixon to be identified as the author of this work has been
asserted by her under the Copyright, Designs and Patents Act 1988.

ISBN 978 1407 19849 1

A CIP catalogue record for this book is available from the British Library.

Printed by CPI Group (UK) Ltd, Croydon, CR0 4YY
Papers used by Scholastic Children's Books are made
from wood grown in sustainable forests.

1 3 5 7 9 10 8 6 4 2

This is a work of fiction. Names, characters, places, incidents
and dialogues are products of the author's imagination or are used
fictitiously. Any resemblance to actual people, living or dead,
events or locales is entirely coincidental.

www.scholastic.co.uk

For my girls,
Azura and Anaya,
who inspire me every
single day.

CHAPTER ONE

RUBY

Sometimes, I dream about being a famous pop star.

I drift off into this crazy, amazing daydream about being someone else, someone glamorous and confident. I imagine stepping out on to a huge stage with spotlights shining down, thousands of fans looking up at me, screaming and cheering as I pick up the microphone and take centre stage, while my backup dancers all take their positions in formation behind me. The stage goes dark dramatically just before the performance begins, and suddenly the music starts up, blasting across the stadium. The crowd erupts with excitement at the first notes of their favourite song. The lights come up and I launch into an incredible dance routine in perfect time with my dancers, before I lift the microphone to my lips and—

SPLAT!

"**AHHHHHHHHHH!**" I scream, leaping to my feet as a huge dollop of mashed potato hits me right in the face. "WHAT THE—"

"Whoops!" My brother Roman sniggers. "Sorry, Ruby, I was aiming for Reggie."

Our scruffy dog, Daisy, comes bounding over from her bed and jumps up at me, barking happily and desperately hoping that the food will drop off my face and on to the floor.

"It was a good throw anyway, though," John comments from the other end of the table, lifting his head from his book long enough to inspect my potato-covered features. "It really hit Ruby in the centre of her face."

"Thanks, John." Roman grins, loading another scoop of mash on to his spoon.

"Can someone pass me a napkin?" I ask, sitting down and pointing at the pile of napkins out of my reach, as Daisy continues to bark at me. "It's gone in my eye!"

"It was a terrible throw," Reggie argues, next to me. "Not that anyone should be surprised. Roman has always been the worst thrower in the family."

"Here we go," Roman sighs. "Jealousy is an ugly quality, Reggie. You really need to get over the fact that

I am by far the higher achieving, more talented, more intelligent twin. Not to mention better looking."

Reggie rolls his eyes. "We're identical."

"I'm still better looking." Roman shrugs. "I have nicer eyes."

"Says who?"

"Says Mum."

"Can someone PLEASE pass me a napkin?" I repeat over Daisy's barking as I attempt to wipe the potato away with my hands. I somehow make it worse, so it's just smearing across my face and all over my eyelashes.

"Mum," Reggie says, ignoring me, "did you tell Roman that he has nicer eyes than me?"

"What, darling?" Mum replies from the top of the table, barely looking up from the manuscript on her lap. "Yes, you can have more potato. Help yourself. Daisy, stop barking, sweetheart, would you?"

"That wasn't my question, Mum." Reggie laughs, shaking his head as Daisy starts barking louder. "Do you think Roman has nicer eyes than I do?"

"You both have beautiful eyes," Mum says, waving his question off and returning her attention to the manuscript. "All my children do. You get them from me."

"Napkin! Please! There is mashed potato in my eye!" I say desperately.

"That's not true, Mum. Jeroame has weird, goggly eyes," Roman teases, getting his spoon lined up, ready to catapult his next dollop of mash across the table.

"I have the eyes of a Greek god," Jeroame replies, typing into his phone. "That's a direct quote from a model scout who came over to speak to me once on the high street."

Reggie snorts. "Yeah, sure."

"Mum, don't I have amazing, model looks?" Jeroame asks with a sly smile.

"Yes, darling, Daisy is a lovely dog," Mum replies on autopilot.

"CAN SOMEONE PLEASE PASS ME A NAPKIN?" I cry out, banging my hand on the table.

"Whoa, calm down," John says, chucking the pack of napkins across the table at me. "You just had to ask."

"Yes, no need to shout, Daisy. I mean, Ruby. Sorry, always getting mixed up," Mum mumbles, scribbling something in the margin of the manuscript, her brow furrowed in concentration.

"But, Mum!" I say in exasperation, wiping the potato out of my eyes. "I asked so many times and no one was listening to me and I really—"

SPLAT!

"Whoops." Roman sniggers as a new dollop of mashed potato slides down my cheek.

Daisy barks ecstatically and jumps up so forcefully, she almost knocks me off my chair.

"Someone really needs to train the dog," John comments, turning a page of his book.

"It's official." Reggie tuts. "Roman, you are the worst thrower in history."

"What about that time you threw the ball into the lake, Reggie?" Jeroame points out.

"That wasn't my fault!" Reggie says.

I reach for another napkin and let out a long sigh as the chaos continues, my brothers all talking and arguing over each other.

This is a daily occurrence.

Being the youngest of six children means that I've grown up in constant noise. Dinner times are the worst. My brothers aren't exactly morning people so they're barely functioning at breakfast, which makes it a much more pleasant dining experience. But in the evenings, when we're all back from school, it reminds me a little of a David Attenborough documentary I once saw about a family of meerkats.

Most of the noise generates from Roman and Reggie, who are identical twins and seventeen years old. They're very outgoing with loads of energy and are both really good at sport. They're in constant competition to be captain of every team, and so far, they have an equal number of trophies. They also love to wind each other up, so a lot of the time they play pranks or challenge each other to do stupid things that end in disaster. Like yesterday when Reggie challenged Roman to slide down the stairs in a laundry basket.

He broke the laundry basket and somehow got his foot stuck in the banister. Reggie threw his head back to laugh loudly and accidentally knocked over a lamp, which smashed everywhere.

Jeroame wasn't laughing. He came out of his room to yell at them for being so loud that he couldn't hear his boss, who was on the phone. Jeroame has left school now; he's nineteen and doing a gap year, gaining experience at a scientific research facility before going to Oxford to study chemistry. Most Friday evenings, he chooses a documentary for us to watch together. Somehow he can retain every bit of information he hears. It's nice to have him still living at home for a bit, especially now that Isabella's left.

Isabella is the eldest. She's twenty-one and at university studying to be a doctor, following in Dad's footsteps. He's a surgeon. I miss Isabella a lot as it was nice having another girl around the house. She always used to yell at the boys when they left their smelly socks lying about and they would listen to her most of the time. None of them ever listen to me, except maybe John.

John is the nearest to me in age, being two years older at fifteen, so, as the second youngest, he kind of understands what it's like to be bottom of the food chain. He doesn't seem to care much about being ignored though; he's happy to do his own thing. Quiet and bookish, John is a lot like Mum: in his own world. He won a BBC writing competition last year for a story he wrote in his free time, and he was on TV and everything. He wants to be a book editor and has already picked up Mum's habit of carrying books wherever he goes, even if it's just to the table for dinner. They even have the same mannerisms. It's spooky.

So, yeah. That's my big, bonkers, high-achieving family. Dad, who's a surgeon; Mum, a renowned book editor; Isabella, a future doctor; Jeroame, a science whizz; Roman and Reggie, sport stars; John, the literary genius; and then there's ... well ... me.

I'm not anything, really. I'm not top of any classes or good at any sports. I have no idea what I want to be when I grow up.

I don't seem to stand out at *anything*.

"Ruby, are you all right, darling?" Mum says suddenly, smiling warmly at me across the table as Roman and

Reggie argue over who gets the last bit of vegetable pie. "You've gone into another one of your dazes."

"When is Ruby not in a daydream?" Dad says suddenly from the doorway, coming over to give me a hug and plant a kiss on the top of my head, making me smile. "And why is there mashed potato all over the table? Daisy even has some on her nose."

We laugh as Daisy goes round and round in circles, desperately trying to shake the potato from her fur and on to the floor.

"How did the operation go?" Mum asks, standing up to greet him.

"It went well. The patient is going to be absolutely fine." He smiles, before noticing the manuscript in her hands. "A future bestseller, I assume?"

"Of course." She grins, giving him a kiss.

We all groan in unison and Roman throws a carrot at them in protest. My parents are very happy together. It's gross.

"Right," Mum says, pulling away from Dad and clapping her hands together, "whose turn is it to clear the table?"

"It's Ruby's turn," Reggie says, jumping up from his seat.

"Yep, definitely Ruby's," Jeroame agrees, following suit.

"What? No, it's not!" I protest, sitting still as everyone else gets up and pushes their chairs under the table, the chair legs screeching loudly and drowning me out. "I did it yesterday! And I really need to go wash the potato off my face."

"Nice try, little sis." Roman laughs, coming over to ruffle my hair. "I can't remember the last time you did any of the chores around the house. Shotgun the remote."

"Yeah, the youngest always gets spoilt," Jeroame says with a cheeky grin. "It's about time you pulled your weight, Rubes. And no chance, Roman, we're watching a science documentary that's on in five minutes."

"HA! Over the football? We'll see about that." Reggie cackles.

"This is SO unfair!" I huff. "Mum! Dad! Tell them."

"Yes," Dad begins, pouring himself a glass of water. "Everyone should—"

But before he can finish his sentence, they all race out of the kitchen in a whirlwind of noise, barging each other out of the way. We hear the TV being switched on, the volume turned up, and then a heated argument break out over the remote, while John's footsteps thud up the stairs to his room.

I'm left at the table on my own.

"Those boys! Don't worry, I'll help you, Ruby," Mum says with a chuckle, shaking her head.

"Me too," Dad says. "We'll get it done in no time and, I promise you, tomorrow, someone else will do it."

"That's what you said yesterday," I say grumpily, getting up and starting to pile the plates.

"Ruby?" Dad says gently.

"Yeah?"

"Well. . ." He pauses. "Did you know that you have mashed potato in your eyebrow?"

When I finish clearing the table and stacking the dishwasher, I head upstairs to my bedroom with Daisy trotting loyally at my feet. Daisy immediately jumps up on to my bed and makes herself comfortable on the duvet while I slump down next to her and stare at all the posters across my wall. They're all of the same person. The most famous person on the planet and my favourite pop star of all time.

Naomi Starr.

Naomi Starr is the BEST singer and dancer ever and she's *crazy* famous even though she's only thirteen years old. I am Naomi's number one fan and have listened to her albums maybe a hundred billion times. Whenever I'm having a bad day, her songs always manage to cheer me up. Hiding away in my room and listening to her music or watching her music videos is basically the only time I ever get to myself, when I can shut out my crazy household.

I know every single lyric and dance move for every one of her songs.

And that's because I secretly spend my spare time dancing along in perfect sync to the choreography of her music videos and singing all the words.

Not that I will ever tell anyone that. I mean, EVER. No one has any idea that I can sing, let alone dance. Except my best friend, Beth, but she has been sworn to secrecy on pain of death. Because it's stupid. I'm only messing around. As I've said to Beth a hundred times, whenever she tries to persuade me to sign up for a school talent show or theatre auditions, it's a silly daydream. I'd never be good enough to be on a stage.

It's just fun to pretend sometimes.

I leave Daisy snoozing on the duvet and prop my phone up against a stack of textbooks on my messy desk. Clicking on Naomi's music video for her new single, I move into the space in the middle of my bedroom floor, excited to learn some new dance moves.

Naomi appears on the screen with her hair styled amazingly, her eyes glittering as she struts towards the camera in an incredible outfit, before she launches into the coolest routine with her backing dancers. I watch her, transfixed, before starting the video again to attempt to learn the first couple of steps. As I move back into the space, I catch a glimpse of myself in the mirror. I'm in my badly fitted school uniform, my hair hasn't been brushed today and I still have a bit of mashed potato in my eyebrow. I look back at Naomi dancing on the screen and sigh. We are worlds apart.

For a moment, I shut my eyes and imagine what it's like to be Naomi Starr.

I bet her life is perfect.

CHAPTER TWO

NAOMI

My life is a **DISASTER**.

I've said that out loud about eight times now, but no one is listening to me. They're all too busy pacing around my Chelsea townhouse sitting room, barking instructions into their phones and completely ignoring any ideas that I might have to sort out this mess.

"Here's your fresh blended juice, Miss Starr," my assistant says, sidling over to where I am lounging on the sofa and holding out a tiny silver tray with a green juice on it. "Your chef made it just how you instructed."

I take the glass, have a sip and then grimace dramatically, plonking the glass right back on that stupidly small tray with a loud clang.

"EW!" I quickly grab the glass of sparkling water

nearby and down it to get the taste out of my mouth. "**GROSS!** Simon, that tastes like . . . I don't even know! But something disgusting!"

"Um . . . it's . . . uh . . . my name is Sam."

"What is even IN that?" I stare at the offending juice on the tray.

"It was all the ingredients that you listed and—"

"Simon, please taste that and tell me what you think," I say, nodding at the juice. "Seriously, have a sip. I need someone else to confirm that it's gross."

He nervously picks up the juice and takes a tiny gulp before wincing and setting it back down. He nods in agreement with me.

"Yeah. It tastes like . . . pondweed."

"Pondweed! That's it. Is Chef trying to kill me?! Ugh, can you take that back and get a new one that doesn't taste like pondweed, please? But still with all those ingredients that I requested before. I read that they are really good for your skin. Thanks."

He scurries off and I watch Mum pace round and round my white carpet along with the rest of my entourage, looking very stressed as she talks into her phone.

I made everyone take off their shoes, so my pristine carpet would be protected from all this pacing, and then had to get Simon to bring in a load of air fresheners to make sure our noses were protected from all these sweaty socks being out in the open.

"There can't be any lilies in the bouquet. No lilies," Mum is saying sternly into the phone, running a hand through her curls. "The recipient, Marina Blair, hates them. And make sure it's the biggest bouquet you've ever created. I mean it, John, make it big." She pauses as John talks on the other end and then her eyes flicker towards me. "Yeah. You'll see what happened in the press. Please get those flowers to her ASAP. Thanks, John, as ever."

She hangs up and then marches over, towering above me and crossing her arms. I pretend not to notice she's there and continue to casually scroll through my phone.

"John is sorting the flowers," she states, frowning. "Hopefully that will smooth things over a little. He's the best florist in London."

"Whatever. Chef just tried to kill me by giving me pondweed in a glass."

She raises her eyebrows. "Are you talking about that juice you asked him to make? You know he spent hours tracking down all those strange, rare ingredients you said just *had* to be in it."

"Simon can back me up here. It was *pondweed*."

"Who's Simon?"

"My assistant."

"His name is Sam."

"Do you think I need a new chef?"

"No, Naomi," Mum sighs, rubbing her forehead. "I think your chef is just fine. You've already changed your chef twice this year."

"Yeah, but I quite like the idea of having a chef who isn't trying to kill me with pondweed disguised as juice."

"Naomi, can we focus on what happened today please? Do you have any idea how much trouble you've caused?"

I shrug.

"Look around the room," Mum says sternly, gesturing behind her. "All of these people in here are working very hard right now to make sure the story doesn't become bigger than it already is. Do you know what's going to happen as soon as the paparazzi print this? We have to do some major damage control."

She sighs again before softening her voice slightly. "You have to start being a bit more responsible. It's tough being in the spotlight all the time, believe me I know, but you have to try."

Mum may be my manager, but she's also a famous pop star herself, or she was back in the day, so she's always making comments like this about how she "gets it" and she knows what it's like to be me.

But she doesn't get it. Nobody gets it. Nobody knows what it's like to be me.

"You do realize that it was an accident, right, Mum?" I point out. "And if it had been anyone else then it wouldn't be a big deal! It's only because it was me. Other teenagers don't have to worry about anything like this. I do one thing wrong and suddenly—"

"Other teenagers don't have number one albums, world tours and thousands of fans who look up to them and count on them to set an example," Mum retorts, shaking her head. "You have to start behaving like a role model."

"Is there any way we can talk about this later? I'm starting to get a migraine from everyone telling me what to do."

"Um, Miss Starr?" My assistant appears with a tray of three different glasses of juice on it this time. "The chef made different blends so you could choose which one you liked best. He deeply apologizes for the ... uh ... pondweed one."

Mum rolls her eyes as I take my time having a sip from each one and swilling the juice in my mouth as though I'm taking it very seriously. If I'm honest they all taste the same to me, but I don't want them to feel as though they've wasted their time, especially as I made a fuss.

"This one is good, thank you," I say, choosing the nearest one. "Also, can you change all the flowers in this room today." I gesture at the various large vases dotted around the room bursting with beautiful, colourful flowers. "I'd like white roses, please. I think they're more calming."

"Absolutely," he says, nodding vigorously. "I'll get those changed at once."

"Thanks, Simon."

"His name is *Sam*," Mum corrects as he hurries off.

"Ms and Miss Starr?" One my publicists comes scurrying over, looking frazzled and holding out her phone. "You asked us to keep you updated. I'm afraid the incident is out. It's all over social media."

Mum looks at the screen and takes a deep breath before clapping her hands loudly.

Everyone in the room immediately stops what they're doing and turns to face her, like an army awaiting instructions from their general.

"All right, team, the story has broken. Things are about to get even crazier. Jennifer, I need you to call every morning breakfast show and book Naomi in for first thing tomorrow to tell her side of the story. Max, I need you to get in touch with your contacts at the major newspapers and offer formal interviews with Naomi. She will be available to journalists in about half an hour and we can give them eight minutes each, no more because she has a rehearsal later for the London concert. Helen, please can you get the hair and make-up team here straight away, along with the stylist as we're going to need different outfits for the various interviews. Make sure they know it's sophisticated looks we're after, nothing too glitzy. And can someone tell Sam to cancel the white roses that Naomi has ordered? The colourful ones are better if any journalists have to come to the house."

She pauses for breath before continuing.

"Mia, can you find a premiere for a children's film that Naomi can attend after her rehearsal this evening? We want her public image to be family-friendly right now. That's important. And, Oliver, we have some free time between morning shows tomorrow morning and our meeting with the record label before rehearsals in the afternoon, so let's make use of it – could we book Naomi in to appear on a radio show? See what you can get me. And we need to know EXACTLY what Marina Blair is going to say about what happened today. I want to be five steps ahead of everyone else involved. Right, that's a good start for now, I think. Does anyone have any questions?"

I raise my hand. She looks at me wearily.

"Yes, Naomi?"

"Hi, yeah, I was wondering when I was going to have a moment to breathe during all this? It kind of feels like you and Chef are in this whole trying-to-kill-me thing together."

"All right, everyone get to work," Mum orders the rest of the room before turning to answer my question. "You know, Naomi, everyone here is trying to protect you. They're working hard for *you*. You're very lucky."

I snort. "Sure. I feel *really* lucky right now. Instead of doing anything *I* want to do, I have to do stuff like justify my mistakes to the world on live television at five a.m. tomorrow morning and spend this evening watching a stupid children's film on my own."

She ignores me, shaking her head and stalking off to chat to the publicity team as they get to work. I look down at my phone and, dreading what's about to come up, I type my name into the search engine. I read the top headline.

CATWALK CALAMITY!

NAOMI STARR ATTACKS MODELS ON THE RUNWAY AND RUINS MAJOR FASHION SHOW!

IS THIS THE POP STAR'S MOST DIVA MOMENT YET?!

My heart sinks. Brilliant. It's all **LIES**. Yeah, I did ruin the fashion show and yes, the whole thing was definitely a calamity, but it was also an ACCIDENT. And I did **NOT** attack any models.

Here's what happened – firstly, I was EXHAUSTED. I got off the plane late last night from a concert I did in Paris and then Mum dragged me out of bed at a ridiculous hour this morning for a photo shoot for *Vogue*, so I only had a few hours' sleep, and then we had to go straight from there to a posh brunch with the CEO of the company launching my next perfume range and who also, by the way, had the craziest eyebrows I've ever seen, so I couldn't concentrate on anything she was saying.

I just stared at her eyebrows. The whole time.

Anyway, I was so dazed and distracted by the eyebrow situation that I forgot to eat anything. Before I knew it, I was ushered out of there to some press conference about a film cameo I did last year, which I can't even remember doing. So, in answer to every question about the role, I had to say stuff like, "Yes, well, you'll have to wait until you see the film," because I genuinely have no idea what the film is, let alone what role I played in it.

That's when I thought enough was enough. My day was getting out of control. So I asked my assistant to give my favourite spa a call and get them to close to the public for the afternoon, so I could go relax in privacy.

But my mum got all grumpy when she heard that and said that I was supposed to be going to Marina Blair's fashion show. According to her it would be a huge insult to not bother turning up.

"You were the one who was going on about this show and how you had to be front row!" Mum said, looking at me strangely. "You told Marina Blair that you would be her guest of honour before she'd even asked!"

So, I went to the show because Mum made me feel guilty, but I was so tired that I can hardly be blamed for what happened when the models took to the catwalk.

Which was . . . I nodded off.

And I must have had some kind of nightmare, because I woke with a start and screamed, throwing the glass of water that had been resting in my hand on my lap right up in the air. The water went everywhere, including over the catwalk, right in the pathway of a model walking down in huge stilettos. . .

Yeah. It didn't end well.

She slipped and fell on her bottom, causing the model walking the other way to trip over her leg and fall on her bottom too. Then, when the models behind them tried to help them up, they slipped and fell as well so it was like a big model pile-up.

And that's when I did the worst thing I could possibly do, according to Mum.

I laughed. Really loudly.

Honestly, I know it looked bad but I couldn't help it! It was like a scene from a sitcom, the way they all kept trying to stand up and slipping all over the place with their long, elegant limbs, like Bambi on ice! It was HILARIOUS.

Anyway, there were all these rules about guests not being allowed phones during the show so no one could put stuff up on social media while it was going on – I don't know why, maybe Marina was trying to be all mysterious and edgy or something – so Mum and I were hoping that MAYBE the story wouldn't leak out.

But obviously someone was breaking Marina's rules. There are all these photos everywhere online of me ruining Marina Blair's fashion show and then *laughing* about it.

Oops.

"Great news!" someone announces from the other side of the room. "I've managed to get Naomi premiere tickets for a children's film tonight. It's called **QUACK-A-DOODLE-DOO: I LOVE YOU!** It's about a duckling who wants to be a cockerel. Attendees have been asked to dress like ducks or cockerels."

"That's PERFECT!" Mum cries, giving her a thumbs up. "A lovely, family-friendly public image. You see, Naomi? Everything is going to be just fine! You're very lucky. Can someone track down a duck or cockerel outfit for Naomi, please? We need it ASAP!"

I slump back on the sofa and bury my head in my designer cushions, wishing I could sink right into them away from here.

Seriously. No one gets what it's like to be me.

CHAPTER THREE

RUBY

"Sorry! Didn't see you there!"

I regain my balance after Noah, one of the most popular boys in school, walks right into my back, knocking all my books out of my hands and sending me stumbling into the wall.

His apology doesn't seem very heartfelt considering he calls it out over his shoulder as he walks away. I rub my arm where it banged against the wall and crouch down to pick up the books that have gone scattering across the floor. Some have already been trodden on by students making their way to class.

"Don't worry about me," I say irritably under my breath, piling up the books. "I'm invisible."

"Let me guess," someone says from above me. "You tripped over your own feet again?"

I smile at Beth's voice and take her outstretched hand so she can help pull me to my feet, while my other arm cradles my now-scuffed books.

"Nope, not this time. Noah barged into me. Apparently, he didn't see me standing here in the middle of the corridor. He didn't even—" I pause, smiling at her appearance. "Hang on. Your hair."

"Yes?"

"It's pink."

"Well observed."

"*Bright* pink."

"VERY bright pink." She runs her fingers through her hair proudly. "You know me. If I'm going to do something, I have to go big."

"You know what, Beth, if anyone can pull off neon-pink hair, it's you. What did your dad say?"

"He's a big fan," she says, giving me a knowing grin. "Just as big a fan as our dear headmaster. Apparently if I don't dye it back, I'm looking at a good few weeks' detention." She shakes her head. "Let me ask you this, Ruby, how is the colour of my hair affecting my academic performance?"

I laugh and fall into step with her as we head down

the corridor to our form room. Beth is my favourite person in the world. We have been best friends ever since I moved to the same road as her when I was six years old. She was instantly fascinated by my big family because she's an only child, raised by her dad.

I still remember her face the first time they popped round for a cup of tea to welcome us to the neighbourhood. They had stepped through the door, ushered in by Mum, only to find themselves right in the middle of pure chaos. We'd just come home from seeing a superhero movie at the cinema and we were all running about the house, pretending to be heroes saving the world from an evil genius, a role played with great enthusiasm by Dad.

"Goodness," Beth's dad, Tim, had said with eyes wide as saucers, "what a big family!"

"Sorry?" Mum had asked, unable to hear him over all the noise.

Roman was jumping from the sofa on to Dad's back with a great war cry, while Reggie and John bounced up and down on the furniture chanting, "Surrender! Surrender!"

"**I SHALL NEVER YIELD!**" Dad had bellowed. "**THE WORLD SHALL BE MINE!**"

The fire alarm had then started going off and we'd

heard Jeroame yell, "Damn it!" from the kitchen as whatever he'd been baking began filling the kitchen with smoke. He'd grabbed a chair and stood on it, fanning around the alarm with a tea towel.

"**HELLO! I'M ON THE PHONE!**" Isabella had then shouted down the stairs, before stomping into her bedroom and slamming the door behind her as loudly as possible.

"I said, what a big family!" Tim had repeated at the top of his lungs.

Beth, meanwhile, had come out from behind him and wandered into the room to get closer to the action. I'd been crouching behind a coffee table ready to leap out at the best opportunity, having fashioned a cape out of one of Jeroame's big jumpers. When I saw Beth standing there, watching us in awe, I took off the jumper and held it out to her.

"Want to play?" I had asked.

She'd nodded, taken the jumper, tied it round her shoulders and then cried out, "**THE WORLD SHALL NEVER BE YOURS!**" before hurtling towards Dad at full speed and rugby-tackling his legs.

We've been best friends ever since and she's spent so much time at our house, it's like she's a member of the family. Her dad is a very busy lawyer and could not be more serious and straight-laced. Beth, on the other hand, is spontaneous, bonkers and loves breaking rules so she can argue why they shouldn't be rules in the first place.

I wish I had half her confidence. She's not afraid of anything.

"Are you going to dye your hair back to its normal colour then?" I ask as she stops to study the school noticeboard. "I don't want to face another term of you in detention all the time. Who else can I hang out with? Please don't get into trouble already."

"I'll think about it," she says, before shooting me a mischievous smile. "But only for you. Not because of what my dad or the headmaster says."

"Is that why you didn't get the bus as normal this morning? Were you dyeing your hair? I messaged you. I thought you'd missed your alarm."

"No, I was actually early for school this morning. I asked Dad to drop me off on his way to the office. Sorry, I meant to text you."

"You were early for school? Why?"

She points at a notice pinned to the board. "That's why."

"*Photographers wanted for the school newspaper. Send your application to the email address below describing why you love photography along with two of your recent photographs*," I read aloud, before turning to her, impressed. "You're applying for the school paper?"

"That's right. You remember that cool camera Dad got me for my birthday? I came in early to get some shots around the school grounds while they were empty."

"Wow! That's amazing. Have you sent your application?"

"Not yet. I will, though." She hesitates and then points to another notice pinned to the school board. "By the way, have you seen this?"

I roll my eyes at her. "Yes, I have."

"And?"

"And what?"

"Come on, Ruby," she says enthusiastically, "the auditions are next Friday, so we'd have this weekend and all next week to put something together. You're not at all tempted?"

"By a talent show? No, Beth, I am not at all tempted."

"I don't understand why you won't even think about it." She sighs. "You could do one of your amazing dance routines and—"

"*Shhh!*" I glance around us nervously. "Someone might hear you!"

"Why is that a bad thing?"

"Because, they would laugh at me," I remind her. "Just

the idea of someone like me entering the school talent show is an absolute joke! Events like that are created for people like—"

"Excuse me!"

I jump as Ali Carlton's voice rings out right behind me. She breezes past us, holding a pen aloft and then flicking her long, glossy red hair behind her shoulders with such gusto that it hits Beth in the face, she writes her name down for the talent show in big, bold letters.

"Oh my god, Ali, this is so exciting," squeals Charlotte, one of her best friends who is standing behind her and clapping her hands. "You are SO going to win, just like every other year. What are you going to sing this time?"

"I'm going to do three songs, I think," Ali replies, clicking her pen triumphantly. "I'll be doing a—"

"A ballad, a West End song and then finishing off the set with an upbeat pop hit," Beth finishes her sentence cheerily. "Just guessing considering that's what you've done every talent show for the past few years. Am I right?"

Ali scowls at Beth. "I haven't decided *exactly* what I'm going to do yet, but it will be different to last year's performance. Maybe I'll do four songs."

"Wow." Beth raises her eyebrows. "Ground-breaking."

"Whatever, Beth – you're just jealous of Ali because she's the best singer in the school," Charlotte snaps.

"How do you know that?" Beth says. "Have you heard everyone in the school sing? Is that what you're telling me? You've heard *every single student* at this school sing? Every single one?"

Charlotte blinks at her. "Well ... no ... but I—"

"Then how do you know Ali is the best? How do you know someone like, oh, I don't know, *Ruby* isn't a better singer?" Beth suggests breezily.

"Who?" Ali asks, confused.

Beth nods at me and they both swivel round, surprised to find me right next to them, as though they've only just noticed I'm there.

"You've never heard her sing, so how do you know she's not better than you, Ali?" Beth continues, having a wonderful time teasing them.

I, however, am **NOT** having a wonderful time. In fact, I've made a mental note to kill Beth as soon as Ali and Charlotte have walked away. Ali stares at me accusingly as though I'm some kind of threat to her talent-show crown.

"She's being hypothetical," I assure her, my voice high and squeaky under her intimidating gaze.

"All I'm saying is you can't go round claiming Ali is

the best singer in the school because she hogs the stage for the majority of the talent show every year," Beth points out.

"I do not hog the stage," Ali huffs. "Mrs Jennings asked me *specially* to do three songs. It's not my problem that no one else is good enough to perform more than one." She narrows her eyes at me. "You can sign up if you want, Ruth. No one is stopping you."

"Oh! Um ... my name is Ruby ... and anyway ... I ... uh ... I didn't—"

"I'm warning you now, though, Ruth," she continues, talking over me, "that the audition process for the talent show is VERY thorough and Mrs Jennings only lets the very best through for the final."

"No, I'm not ... I'm not signing up ... it was—"

"What did you do to your hair?" Ali asks Beth, wrinkling her nose. "Why is it so ... pink?"

Beth shrugs. "I wanted to do something different."

"It looks stupid," Ali states, before her lips curl into a thin smile. "Maybe that could be your talent for the show, Beth. How to look ridiculous."

Looking very smug, Ali then marches away from the noticeboard and down the corridor, with Charlotte sniggering and hurrying to catch her up. Beth doesn't look embarrassed or upset at all; she looks amused.

"This is why we need you to sign up to the talent show, Ruby," she says as we watch them saunter off. "Otherwise we're going to have to sit through the Ali Show, like every year. On behalf of the school, I'm begging you: please sign up and show everyone how talented and amazing you are! I've seen you, Ruby. All you need is more confidence and belief in yourself. You are *brilliant* at singing and dancing."

"Good try, but it's never going to happen. Thanks for saying nice things, though," I say firmly, right before the bell rings, signalling the start of lessons. "Come on, we have to go."

"Double maths first thing in the morning," Beth groans as I usher her down the corridor. "It's a form of torture, especially on a Friday. Mr Jones always picks me to answer questions and he never picks you; it's so unfair."

"What can I say?" I cling on to my books as someone coming the other way barges past me, almost knocking them to the ground again. "Sometimes it's good to be invisible."

CHAPTER FOUR

NAOMI

"You're late. Again."

I sigh dramatically at Mum's cranky tone.

"Mum, I JUST walked through the door," I say, taking off my sunglasses with a flourish. "Any chance you can give me five seconds before beginning the daily lecture? It's the weekend."

"Is this a joke to you?" She gestures around the studio at all the people sitting in clusters around the edges. My choreographer, Martin, is standing next to her looking furious. "All of your dancers have been here, patiently waiting for you, for two hours. You've wasted their time! Do you understand how rude that is?"

"I texted you to say I was going to be a bit late," I point

out. "It wasn't my fault! I slept through my alarm because I was exhausted from yesterday—"

"Which I predicted would happen," Mum interrupts, folding her arms. "That's why I woke you up and then witnessed you getting out of bed. So no excuse there."

"I wasn't finished!" I huff, handing my bag to Simon, who is standing awkwardly behind me and looking very nervous about this confrontation. He should really be used to it by now. "As I was saying, I was slightly delayed because I was EXHAUSTED from the billion events I attended yesterday, including all the rehearsals here, so it took me a little longer to get ready. Then the car was late—"

"Nice try, but I saw Kelly arriving to pick you up as I left the house to come here early and make sure everything was ready. She was there at eight a.m. as requested."

"Again, let me finish! I was going to say, the car was late *to leave the house*. Honestly, Mum, no offence but you're not a very good listener."

For a moment I think I may have gone too far as her jaw clenches, her eyes go all wide and that weird vein on her forehead becomes VERY prominent, but then she closes her eyes, takes a long, deep breath and, in a strangled voice that doesn't even sound like her, says, "Go on."

"Thank you," I say graciously. "So as I was saying, the car was late to leave the house because this cat came and

36

sat in front of it on the driveway and would **NOT** go away. Isn't that right, Simon?"

"Um ... yeah ... that did actually happen," he squeaks.

"Thank you for confirming, *Sam*," Mum says pointedly.

Whoops. In my defence, he really does look much more like a Simon than a Sam.

"Sorry, Sam," I say over my shoulder, before turning back to Mum. "We all tried to move the cat but it kept trying to scratch us! It was really angry. Simon ... I mean, Sam had to go get salmon from Chef to lure it away. Then once we set off, I asked Kelly to stop for coffee but she forgot I hate that place on the corner near ours and I was dozing so didn't notice till AFTER she'd got the coffee. **BLEUGH**, that coffee is disgusting and way too hot. I burnt my tongue last time, do you remember?"

Mum purses her lips. I take that as a yes and continue.

"Anyway, I had to get her to throw that sludge away. That's when I remembered how good the coffee is in the café in Harrods. So I asked Kelly to head there and then we came straight here. It was only a small diversion."

"So why are you SO LATE?!"

"Because I popped upstairs to the shop floor *just in*

case they'd had the new Chanel drop and guess what? It had just arrived! Such perfect timing! Wait until you see the cute jacket I've bought."

Mum shakes her head while Martin gives me such a disapproving look that I begin to bubble with rage. This is so not my fault. If Mum and my PR team hadn't forced me to go to that awards ceremony last night, then I might have been a little more with it this morning.

But no, I HAD to go because I was nominated for Most Popular Performer, or whatever. It was so boring. And I have two of those awards already, so it's not like it was a big deal.

I'm sorry, but the least people can do is understand that if I'm going to be forced to make an appearance at all these events, then I need good coffee that is brewed just how I like it.

"Come on, I'm here now!" I announce grumpily to the studio, fed up of talking to Mum, who has put me in a bad mood. "Shall we get to work?"

The dancers leap to their feet and hurry to get into formation. I put my bag down and take off my hoodie, ready to begin my stretches.

"We'll talk about your attitude later," Mum seethes, walking past to take her place at the side of the studio.

I don't say anything and roll my eyes at my reflection

in the mirror facing me. I really could use a break from Mum and her constant, boring nagging. What is the big deal? So, I'm a couple of hours late. We have the studio booked for the whole day; it's not like the dancers have anywhere better to be! They probably had a lovely time sitting around and relaxing while they waited. They're being paid! This is their JOB.

As I roll my shoulders and Martin sets up the music, I watch a group of dancers whispering behind me in the mirror. I notice them all glance at me slyly and then snigger.

I look down at my feet, pretending to focus on my warm-up and trying to ignore the sudden pang in my chest.

It's happened before, that pang. I don't know why I even care, but any time I ever rehearse for a concert or a music video, my backup dancers are always talking and laughing during breaks but never bother to include me.

Not that I *want* to be included. Obviously. I make that very clear.

I'm way too busy to stand around chatting or whatever. What would I have to talk about with anyone else anyway? My life is SO different from theirs.

It's just, sometimes I wonder what it would be like if one of them came over to say hi. Whether it might be fun to have someone to high-five after we nail the routine, like they always do.

After a rehearsal for a concert I did in London last year, I was being escorted to my car by my bodyguards when I noticed the dancers and the band heading out together.

"Where are they going?" I had asked Mum, stopping at the car door while she typed into her phone.

"Who?"

"The people in the show. The musicians and dancers," I'd said, pointing them out. "I think I can see Martin with them, too."

"They're going for dinner," she'd replied.

"Oh. All of them? Together?"

"Yes."

I'd hesitated. "Was I invited?"

That's when Mum looked up, confused. "You're busy tonight. You have an album launch to get to before—"

"I know, but was I *invited* to the dinner? I don't remember anyone mentioning it and, I don't know." I'd shrugged, trying to act casual and swallow the lump in my throat. "We've all been working together a couple of weeks and I was there all day today. . . It seems odd that no one said anything or thought to invite me."

"Naomi," Mum had said, sharing a look with my PA at the time, Mel, "if you want to be invited to things, maybe you could try talking to people in rehearsals. . ."

"What would I talk to them about?"

"Whatever you like. You could ask them about themselves or whether they enjoy your songs or thank them for all the hard work they put in."

"Why don't they ask *me* any of those things? Why don't *they* put in the effort?" I'd pointed out defensively. "Whatever, I don't care. I'm too busy for stupid dinners with friends. I have number-one albums to promote."

And with that, I'd slid into the car, putting on my sunglasses so no one would notice that I was blinking back tears. It was so stupid of me to care. I'd stared out the window, comforting myself with the fact that they all wanted to be me. I was Naomi Starr and, like I'd said, I didn't have time for boring dinners with ordinary people who didn't even have the manners to invite me.

Despite reminding myself of all that, I got the stupid pang then, too.

Oh, and to make things worse, that PA, Mel, ended up selling stories about me to the press, including one about how I refused to talk to my dancers because they were so beneath me and then got upset when they didn't invite me to hang out with them.

Which is exactly why I don't make an effort to get to know my dancers or crew.

I can't trust anyone.

"OK, into positions!" Martin instructs across the dance studio, clapping his hands together loudly and jolting me from my memory. "No messing around today; the concert is on Monday! Let's go from the top of 'Shining Bright'."

I groan without thinking. Martin shoots me a look.

"Everything OK, Naomi?" he asks in a strained voice.

"Yeah, I just thought we'd got 'Shining Bright' perfect yesterday. We did the routine about a hundred times."

"Well, just to be sure, I'd like to start with that one. Especially as it's your opening song."

"Fine. But I thought 'Attention Please' needed more practice. And I also wanted to talk to you about the choreography to 'Am I Wrong?' because I'm not sure that introduction works. I was thinking about it last night and I think we should change it."

Mum clears her throat loudly, but I ignore her.

"I thought we'd agreed the introduction choreography to 'Am I Wrong?' was perfect," Martin says, looking pained. "It's quite late in the day to change it now, don't you agree?"

Here's the thing. I really don't like Martin's voice.

I know that's not a nice thing to say but the truth is, I have to listen to it all the time and it's very whiny and grating. I asked Mum the other day if maybe it's time

42

to consider a new choreographer who doesn't have such an annoying voice, but she narrowed her eyes at me and went, "I'm going to pretend you didn't just say that."

Which is a weird reply to a very reasonable point.

"I know it's late to change it," I say, my hands on my hips. "But I'm the one up on the stage dancing in front of thousands of people, not you, Martin. I want to be happy with MY performance to MY song."

He inhales deeply and attempts a smile. "I see. Well, I guess it's a long day ahead, then. Nothing we can't handle."

"Actually, I can't stay all day."

"*Excuse me*?" Martin squeaks, his voice so high-pitched it hurts my ears.

"I have a spa appointment this afternoon so we only have the morning to get this sorted."

He swivels to face Mum, who is now marching over to join the conversation.

"We only have the morning?" he asks Mum, glancing at the clock on the wall. "And we have already lost two hours!"

"Naomi, I don't have anything in the schedule about a spa appointment. You're here all day to rehearse for tomorrow night's concert."

"But, Mum, you said that if I—"

43

"I said I would book you something for tonight if you needed to relax after a full day rehearsing!"

She's practically yelling now, making everyone in the room stop what they're talking about to stare at us.

"Honestly, Naomi," she continues, the forehead vein taking on a life of its own, "I don't know what has got into you but I'm tired of it!"

"Mum, this is my concert! Why can't I have any say in how I perform my songs? It doesn't seem fair that—"

"You know what's not fair? Turning up two hours late!" she cries. "Why were you late? Because you drove across the city for one cup of coffee! Coffee, Naomi! And the day before a big concert, you want to change the choreography, hours of work that Martin and your dancers have put in! Do you really think that is acceptable behaviour?"

"I know it's last minute."

"We can't change the choreography now," Martin barks. "We just can't!"

"I don't see why not," I say, a little shocked at Martin's tone. "I have some cool ideas. If we at least tried—"

"Naomi, what is WRONG with you?" Mum shouts, throwing her arms up in the air.

The room falls silent. I stare at her. A couple of the dancers shift uncomfortably. Martin clenches his jaw.

Simon, still holding my bag, stares firmly at the floor, a deep shade of crimson creeping up his neck.

I don't say anything for a moment, seething that she's shouted at me in front of everyone like I'm a little child. Then, I make a decision. I take a deep breath and turn to Martin.

"Sorry. Let's begin the rehearsal."

Mum and Martin share a look as I move into my position, front and centre of the floor. I refuse to make eye contact with Mum or reply to any of Martin's "well done" or "nice work, Naomi" comments for the whole morning. I do all the dance steps perfectly.

When we take a five-minute break, I head out of the studio saying I'm popping to the bathroom.

Then, I walk down the flight of stairs, past reception and through the revolving doors out of the building and into the waiting car parked right outside the exit.

"Time for my spa appointment, Kelly," I tell her, slamming the door behind me.

"Naomi! I thought Riley said you were in rehearsals for the whole day," Kelly says, putting her book down and swivelling round in the driver's seat to face me.

I put on my sunglasses and flash her a wide, innocent grin. "Change of plans."

CHAPTER FIVE

RUBY

NAOMI STARR PREPARES TO TAKE CENTRE STAGE IN LONDON

The pop star looked happy and calm this
afternoon, pictured here heading into
the arena where she will be performing
in front of thousands of fans tonight.
When tickets went on sale a few months
ago, they sold out in record time.

"Naomi is excited to be performing
in front of her home crowd and has been
rehearsing tirelessly for weeks," a source close
to the star said. "She's looking forward to
putting all the recent drama behind her."

Miss Starr has recently been at the centre
of some bizarre diva scandals, including last
week when she disrupted designer Marina
Blair's exclusive fashion show. Reports
came through yesterday that she stormed
out of concert rehearsals because a dancer
ate her bagel. We have contacted Naomi
Starr's representatives for comment.

"You know," Beth says, nudging me in the ribs with her
elbow, "you get an embarrassingly dopey smile on your
face whenever you read anything to do with Naomi Starr."

"No, I don't!"

"Yes, you do." She laughs. "I can always tell when
you're on her Instagram or when you're reading the latest
updates about her. You go all dreamy and wistful."

"I do **NOT** go all dreamy and wistful. I like reading
about her life, that's all."

Beth smiles mischievously. "And wistfully dreaming
of being her?"

"Well, wouldn't it be cool to be someone like Naomi
Starr and have no problems?" I point out, putting my
phone away before I drop it. "I bet she doesn't have to get
squished into a bus like a sardine. I told you we should
have waited for the next one to come along."

We're jolted forward as the bus brakes and I slam into the armpit of the person standing next to me. He glares at me before "accidentally" standing on my toes as the bus accelerates again, sending us jolting back. My eyes water with the pain.

"You're saying you'd rather be driven about in a spacious limo with darkened windows and posh heated seats than be squeezed into the standing-room-only crowd of a London bus, rammed with people who have all got soaked in the rain waiting for it to come along?" Beth rolls her eyes, her cheek squashed against a handrail. "You are such a diva."

The bus comes to a sudden stop and the doors fling open. My foot is trodden on several more times and someone's wet umbrella hits Beth's cheek as people quickly bustle past to get out.

"Well, that's disgusting," she comments, wiping the droplets of rain and speckles of dirt off her face. "But at least we have some space now."

It's such a popular stop that some seats have become available. Once the doors close and the driver sets off, Beth and I carefully make our way down the bus to two free spaces at the back.

"Lovely." Beth grimaces, feeling the seats before she plonks herself on one. "They're soaking wet from people's coats. Prepare to look as though you've peed yourself when you get up."

"I wish I'd got tickets for Naomi's concert tonight," I comment, sitting down next to her. "I was in the queue online for ages."

"She'll add another date," Beth assures me. "We'll get them next time."

"I am SO excited for Naomi Starr's concert tonight!" a voice exclaims loudly from the seats in front of us. "*Everyone* is going! Our whole crew!"

I hadn't even noticed Ali sitting in front of us next to Noah. I feel an ache when I see her holding up her phone to show Noah her ticket.

"We've got amazing seats too," she adds, pointing out the row letter to him.

"Cool," he replies, sounding bored. "I can't remember which ones are her songs."

"Oh my god, Noah, her songs are the BEST ones! Don't worry, you can sit next to me – I know all the lyrics, so I'll be singing along to every one!"

"Wow, lucky you, Noah," Beth says under her breath.

I stifle a laugh but Ali heard Beth's muttering and she swivels round in her seat.

"Oh. It's you." She sniffs. "Are you going to the concert tonight?"

"Sadly not," Beth sighs, while I stare down at my shoes, "so we'll be missing out on both your and Naomi Starr's singing."

"Shame you didn't get tickets. Have fun sitting alone at home," Ali beams, flicking her hair over her shoulder smugly. "Oh and Ruth—"

"Her name is Ruby," Beth corrects, scowling. "You're in several classes with her."

Ali ignores her and pulls out an envelope from her bag, handing it to me. "Here."

I glance at Beth wondering what on earth is going on but she looks as baffled as I feel, so I pull out the thick, black card inside. It's an invitation.

"Your birthday party?" I ask in awe, staring at the gold lettering and the star decoration around the sides. Beth's jaw has dropped open. "Are you serious?"

"Yeah, it's the Saturday after the talent show final and the theme is stars," Ali says excitedly. "I'm obviously going as Naomi Starr."

I'm lost for words. I can't believe Ali Carlton is inviting me to her birthday party. I'm *never* invited to birthday parties, except for Beth's, and they usually just involve me going round to her house with Daisy to watch movies. Obviously, I'll be asking Ali if Beth can come too, because I would be terrified of going on my own, but the fact that someone as popular as her has noticed me and wants me to be at her party makes me feel so excited.

Maybe I'm not that invisible after all!

"Wow!" I finally say, gripping the invitation tightly as though it might disappear. "Thank you!"

"Cool." Ali smiles. "So if you could tell him to get a star-themed costume that would be great."

I snap my head up. "Him?"

"Yeah, your brother. John. A couple of years above us. He is your brother, right?"

"Um. Yeah. Yeah, John's my brother."

"That's what Charlotte said after we bumped into you at the noticeboard yesterday. So, I figured you could pass on the invitation to him at home or whatever. I was going to try to give it to him today at school but he wasn't around when I handed them out to his friends. I think one of them said he was writing something up for the paper." She smiles, tilting her head slightly. "He is so geek chic. It's adorable. Anyway, if you could give that to him I'd really appreciate it."

"This invitation is for John," I say slowly, realization dawning on me. "You ... you want me to pass it on to John, my brother."

"Yeah." She gives me a strange look. "You don't mind, right?"

Beth shifts uncomfortably in her seat next to me. She knows exactly what's just gone through my head and I can't bear that she's aware of my mistake. My cheeks begin to burn with embarrassment. I'm so stupid. Ali doesn't even get my name right, so why would she be inviting me to her party? People like me do NOT get invited to Ali Carlton's parties.

"Yeah, of course," I croak, shoving the invitation back in its envelope and into my bag. "I'll make sure he gets it."

"This is my stop," Ali announces, getting to her feet. "Come on, Noah. Everyone is meeting at my house so my parents can take us to the concert. We don't want to be late! This is going to be so much FUN!"

I watch her flounce off the bus, Noah in tow, and put up a pink, glittery umbrella before she links her arm through his and they head off down the road, laughing.

"You OK?" Beth asks gently.

"Yeah. Why wouldn't I be?"

"She did that on purpose," she says accusingly. "I know she did. She could have said it was for John as soon as she gave it to you, or asked one of his friends to pass it on."

"It's fine. I was being stupid."

"Her party is going to suck anyway. How about the night of her party, we do something really cool? Like, find out where Naomi Starr is going to be and then get a picture with her. Can you imagine Ali's face if she saw that?"

I smile warmly at her. I don't deserve Beth.

"That sounds great." I pull myself to my feet using the handrail as the bus begins to slow to the next stop. "I'm getting off here."

Beth frowns. "We're two stops away from home."

"I'm heading to the library for a bit," I say, giving her a wave.

"Have fun, nerd!" she calls out after me as I make my way down the bus.

The doors fling open and I step out right into the middle of a deep puddle.

"ARGH!"

I jump on to the pavement but it's too late. My shoes are sopping wet and the cold water seeps into my socks. I even hear the driver chuckling to himself as the doors close behind me and the bus pulls away. Then, while I'm standing in the pouring rain, I go to get my umbrella and realize I've left it on the bus.

"Oh, **COME ON**!" I yell out to no one before legging it towards the library.

The public library near where I live is my favourite place to go when I've had a bad day. It's so peaceful and quiet, the complete opposite to home. I can think in there. And the librarian, Rose, is really nice and welcoming. She has dark, curly hair and big, round glasses, and always wears brightly coloured scarves.

"Hello, Ruby!" She beams at me as I burst through the door, my hair plastered to my face from the rain. "Oh dear. Forgot your umbrella today? And a coat from the looks of it."

"I left my umbrella on the bus."

"Well, you can dry off in here. It's nice to see you! No one has come in all afternoon. So, how have you been? How's school?"

I push my hair back from my forehead and come over to her desk, which is a jumble of books and paper.

"Fine, thanks."

She peers at me through her glasses. "What's wrong?"

"Nothing's wrong," I say, shrugging. "I need a book for my history homework on—"

"Ruby" – she holds up her hand – "something is up, I can tell. You've lost your usual . . . spark."

"I don't have a spark."

"Yes, you do! You have a wonderful, bright spark. But you're trying to hide it today. Why?"

I shake my head at her, smiling. "You're mad."

"Always." She grins. "Come on, tell me what's up."

"It's nothing, really. Sometimes I feel . . . invisible. My friend, Beth, says I need to have more confidence, but it's hard to feel confident when people who are in the same class as you can't even remember your name, right?"

"Yes, it is hard," Rose agrees. "I wonder whether you need a little help in seeing yourself."

"Seeing myself? What are you talking about? I can already see myself in a mirror or whatever."

"Not quite what I meant," she chuckles, opening one of the desk drawers and pulling out a hardback book. She holds it out to me. "Here."

I take the book and look at the title on the cover in bold, swirly writing: **HOW TO SHINE**.

"What is this?" I ask, turning it over to read the back. "I've never seen it before."

"It's an unusual book I found a long time ago; there aren't many copies around but I'm lucky enough to have got my hands on two. I found it very helpful and I think you will, too. It's all about growing in confidence and believing in yourself. Give it a try and let me know what you think of it. Lots of tips and good advice in there."

"Thanks so much, Rose." I study the front cover. It looks old and a bit outdated. "You really think reading this will help me?"

"Worth a shot. I found it useful." She shrugs. "It

helped me to see that when you have faith in yourself, anything can happen."

"Really? Like what?"

Suddenly, the door to the library swings open with such force, it hits the wall with a bang.

A girl marches in wearing large sunglasses, her clothes completely soaked through. I gasp, dropping the book when I look up and see who it is.

Naomi Starr.

CHAPTER SIX

NAOMI

I'm in trouble. Big trouble.

And to make matters worse, I'm completely lost and in some kind of library that smells like dust and looks like it was last decorated in the 1950s.

Ew.

"I need a car," I inform the woman behind the desk, who is blinking at me through thick-rimmed glasses. "As soon as possible. Thank you."

There's a girl standing next to the librarian's desk staring at me open-mouthed. I pretend not to notice her. She's clearly star-struck and I have no time for crazy fans right now.

"Excuse me?" the librarian says, raising her eyebrows.

"A car, please. Right away." I take my sunglasses off

to look her right in the eye so she knows that I'm not in the mood for any dawdling.

"I'm afraid this is a library. Not a taxi service. But I can direct you to the nearest bus stop or taxi rank."

"Look," I begin, trying to be as patient as possible, "I need a car urgently and I can't go wandering around or waiting at a bus stop, OK? The paparazzi will be surrounding this place any minute because I saw someone take a photo of me as I got off the bus and, trust me, it never takes them long to track me down once it's up on social media. I don't have my phone so I need you to call me a car. *Please*. It's an emergency."

The librarian inhales deeply and then says, "All right, let me see if I can call a local taxi company," before disappearing into a small office behind her.

The girl in front of the desk slowly bends down to pick up the book that she dropped and then continues to stare at me. I'm used to people going weird around me, so I simply ignore her, focusing instead on how I'm going to get to the car once it arrives without the press getting photos of my hair looking this bad thanks to the pouring rain.

This is a nightmare. I wasn't lying to the librarian when I said it is an emergency. It really is.

I knew when I woke up this morning that it was going

to be a bad day. Mum and I had a huge fight last night when I got back from the spa.

"How COULD you?!" she kept saying over and over. *"How could you?"*

Like I'd done something really bad. But why was it such a big deal? I proved yesterday morning that I knew the dance steps perfectly, so it's not like I needed to rehearse any more. And if they weren't interested in any of my new ideas for performing MY songs, then why was it so important for me to be there? The backing dancers could rehearse without me no problem. I was so angry at her for yelling at me in front of everyone.

"I needed a BREAK!" I told her, storming up the stairs. "Everyone tells me what to do all the time and I felt **TRAPPED.**"

"Your concert is tomorrow night, Naomi!" she cried back, coming up the stairs after me.

I slammed the bedroom door behind me but she came waltzing in. She has no respect for my privacy.

"You really let me down today. Do you know how worried I was when I didn't know where you were?"

"Oh please, Mum. I told Kelly to let you know that I was fine and didn't want to be disturbed."

"And what about Martin?" she growled, folding her arms.

"What about Martin?"

"He is freaking out, Naomi! He wanted to rehearse all day! What about the dancers? Everyone is terrified about the concert tomorrow! You're performing in front of thousands of people! You have to be prepared!"

"Mum, you are *really* disturbing my Zen," I told her calmly, sitting down on my silk sheets. "Please leave and shut the door behind you."

She exhaled and then said in a quiet, gentler voice, "It's a busy time for you right now and I need you to be dedicated. I know it's hard work – I remember what it was like when I was doing world tours and I felt like I didn't have time to breathe! But this is what you have to do to succeed in this industry. Please don't pull a stunt like today ever again. It's not fair on anybody."

"And what about what's fair on me?" I pulled my eye mask on and settled into my squishy pillows. "As I said, I needed a break."

"About the concert tomorrow. . ."

"It will be fine, Mum. Don't worry," I assured her, which I thought was very kind of me considering I was angry at her for completely ruining the calm aura I'd achieved at the spa. "Everything will be fine."

But I was wrong. Very wrong. It was **NOT** fine.

This morning I was woken up at an OBSCENE

hour. Mum came barrelling through the door, turned on the lights and then in came Simon with a cup of coffee, already looking apologetic.

"What's happening?" I said, bleary-eyed and dazed. "Is the house on fire?"

"What? Why would the house be on fire?" Mum said chirpily, drawing back the curtains.

"Because why else would I need to be up at four a.m.?" I replied, having pulled my eye mask up and examined the time on my phone.

"You have rehearsals this morning."

"*What*? No, I don't. We don't have sound testing until this afternoon."

"Well, the plans changed when you decided to skip almost an entire day of rehearsals yesterday," she said in a strained tone. "There's a lot to do and we only have today to do it, now."

I groaned, put my eye mask back on and pulled the duvet over my head. "No."

She came to sit down on the edge of my bed and gently pulled the duvet away. "Naomi, I know it's been a bit crazy recently and I was thinking about it last night. You're right."

I lifted my eye mask to peer at her. "Huh?"

"You're right. You deserve a break. You've had a lot on."

"You . . . you're agreeing with me?"

"I thought we could make a deal."

"I'm listening."

"If you get up now, work hard at the rehearsals today and the concert tonight, I will cancel *everything* for tomorrow. You can have the day off and you can do whatever you like. I'll book out the spa for you or we can go shopping . . . whatever you want to do. Up to you."

I sat up, not sure if this was some kind of joke. I couldn't remember the last time I'd had a day off.

"Are you serious?"

"Yes," she said. "It will be good for you to relax before the concert in Berlin. But you also have a lot of people counting on you today, including all your fans, so I need you to give your all. What do you think?"

I pretended to think about it for a second. "All right. Deal."

I jumped out of bed then, ready to get to work. I haven't been able to make any decisions for myself for a long time and the idea of having a day off to do whatever I wanted sounded *perfect*.

And everything had been going to plan. I was on time for rehearsals and I didn't complain *too* much about how early it was. I put up with Martin's grating voice and only yelled back at him a couple of times; I didn't send back the disgusting lunch that Simon got me, even though I could barely eat it; I was patient throughout the HUNDREDS of boring soundchecks; I only complained once about the lighting checks taking years to complete; I didn't say anything when my costume designer pinched my skin by accident as she made a last minute adjustment to one of my dresses for the concert; and I even held back when my make-up artist finished my look for tonight's show.

"What do you think?" she said when she was done.

I thought it was TERRIBLE. The eyeliner was wonky, the eyeshadow was the wrong shade and she'd decided to "mix it up" by choosing a new lip colour. She had chosen badly.

"Naomi, you look **FANTASTIC**," Mum said, beaming at me from her chair.

My mum is a very good liar.

Anyway, I put up with ALL of that because of the deal I'd made with Mum. I held up my side of the bargain. And then, as I was starting my vocal warm-ups, it all went wrong.

"Can I speak to you for a moment?" Mum asked sheepishly, pulling me away from the piano and my vocal coach.

"Do you think I sound flat? I think I sound flat. Can someone get me a water? Simon! Can you get me a water, please? I sound flat. Simon! Wait! Can I also get a sparkling elderflower? Quickly, please, my throat is dry."

"Naomi, you sound great," Mum assured me. "About tomo—"

"And can you have a word with the sound guys?" I sighed. "The earpiece was SO uncomfortable in rehearsals; I'm sure they didn't fit it right. Honestly, you'd think in an arena this big they'd have professionals working here."

"Naomi, I need you to concentrate. About your day off tomorrow. . ."

I knew what she was about to say before she said it, and I stepped back from her.

"No! You promised! We made a deal."

"I know and I'm so sorry!" She sounded genuinely upset but that wasn't the point. "I've tried everything to move this meeting with your record label tomorrow, but they really can't do it any other time. There's a few people who need to be there and we are being very unsuccessful trying to coordinate calendars for everyone."

"NO. I am not working tomorrow! That's that."

"It's one meeting and I promise you have the rest of the day off."

"Mum! No! It's not fair!" I huffed. "Everyone else gets days off!"

"You are going to have time off! I'll make it up to

you, all right? I've tried everything I can," she claimed, exasperated. "Just one meeting and that's it."

"**I SAID NO!**"

"Um, Ms Starr?" One of the stage crew approached us awkwardly. "I'm so sorry to interrupt, but we really need to run a few things by you before the show. Is it all right if you come with me now? We don't have much time."

"Yes, of course." Mum nodded, before turning back to me. "I'll be back in a bit."

I pursed my lips and didn't say anything. She followed him out of the room and my vocal coach had cleared her throat.

"Naomi? You want to start from where we left off?"

"NO! I need some air," I snapped, grabbing my sunglasses before marching right out of there.

I felt a bit bad for being so sharp with my vocal coach. It wasn't her fault that everything in my life is a big mess. I shouldn't have taken it out on her but I was so CROSS. Is it too much to ask to have some time to myself when I work so hard? And, HELLO, but I highly doubt anyone at the record label is as busy as I am. They should work around my schedule and do the meeting another time!

I stormed out of the stage doors into the back alley, put my sunglasses on and leaned against the wall. I didn't even care that it was pouring with rain. I felt so overwhelmed and angry with everything, I wanted to cry. And I NEVER cry. I tried to breathe deeply like that beauty therapist at the spa had told me to do yesterday.

"Goodness! You are very tense," she'd said as she started my hot stone back massage. "You need to relax."

I'd wanted to shout, **WHY DO YOU THINK I'M HERE AT THE SPA, GENIUS?!** but instead just went, "Mmm."

It was when I was doing my breathing exercises in that back alley and spotted a bus approaching on the main road that a thought flitted across my brain: *I could just walk away from here and hop on that bus.*

I could get away. Be on my own for a bit. Have some quiet. I never, ever felt quiet. There was always chaos around me. Everywhere I went. There were always people speaking, doing their jobs, on their phones, telling me where I needed to be, what I needed to be doing, what I should be saying and to whom I should be saying it.

I could get on that bus and get away from it all.

Without any more thought, I ran for it.

With my full show make-up on, I darted down the alley towards the main road through the rain and jumped on the bus just in time before it pulled away. No one recognized me and I managed to get a seat by the window, tucked away at the back. I took my sunglasses off as I figured it would draw more attention to have them on when it was raining. I sat there, looking out the window, watching the arena fall into the distance. I leaned back in the seat and let out a sigh of relief.

I sat on the bus for ages, feeling very pleased with myself for taking a stand. I posted a quote on my Instagram the other day about standing up for yourself. It had got millions of likes. That's exactly what I felt I was doing. Standing up for myself.

But obviously, I couldn't sit on the bus for ever. And then I started to feel a bit bad because I didn't have my phone on me and I didn't want Mum to panic. *Then* I noticed the time on someone's watch who was standing up near me.

I'd missed the start of the concert.

At first, my throat closed up and my whole body tensed. But then I reminded myself that this was what I'd been aiming for when I walked out of the arena. I'd wanted to give them all a shock. Maybe they'd start listening to me for once.

Anyway, I got off the bus when I noticed a huddle of girls on some seats ahead gasping and pointing their phones unsubtly at me, and now here I am in this library, the first place I wandered into, desperate to go home.

"I'm your biggest fan," the girl says so quietly, I can

barely hear her.

"Yeah, well, I'm not in the mood for my biggest fan right now," I reply sharply.

She immediately hangs her head, looking mortified. I feel guilty and I open my mouth to explain that it's not her fault or anything, I'm just under a lot of stress right now, when the librarian reappears.

"I've ordered you a taxi from a local company. They'll be here any second now."

"Great."

I put my sunglasses back on and peer through the window of the door. The rain is slowing now and becoming more of a drizzle. I can make out a huddle of people hurrying down the road. Cars are pulling up and parking on the road too, with drivers getting out, cameras hanging from their necks.

"The paparazzi is here," I say out loud to myself. "I *knew* they would be."

I bite my lip as they begin to gather around the library in a crowd, chatting to each other and checking their cameras. I REALLY don't want them to get a photo of me looking like a drowned rat. I'm giving them a lot of material today. A no-show at my own concert and then hiding in a library, not exactly looking my best.

A car drives up the road and parks badly in front of

the entrance. It's a taxi.

"Right, time to go." I turn to the others. "I need something to shield my face."

"What?" The librarian looks baffled.

"Something to shield my face from the reporters!" I say impatiently. "A newspaper or something. Hurry! The crowd is getting bigger out there!"

She begins looking around her desk but it's an absolute tip. I don't have all day.

"Just give me that," I say angrily, reaching out and snatching the book from the hands of the girl claiming to be my biggest fan.

It's not ideal, but it will have to do. I take a deep breath and open the doors, keeping my head bowed and holding up the book to shield my face as the camera flashes start going off like crazy. I reach the door handle, fling it open and jump in the taxi, yelling, "**DRIVE! DRIVE!**"

The driver puts his foot down and we hurtle down the road, away from the reporters.

"Wow!" the driver says, looking in his rear-view mirror. "Are you *Naomi Starr*?"

"Yes, I am," I reply, leaning back and pushing my sunglasses up my nose. "But right now, I really wish I wasn't."

CHAPTER SEVEN

RUBY

"TIME TO GET UP, RUBY!"

I wake with a start at Mum's voice and her sharp knocking on my bedroom door. I realize I fell asleep last night reading and my face is stuck to one of the pages. I carefully peel it off and then nestle down into my pillow again, hoping to get five more minutes.

But Mum's left the door ajar and Daisy comes bounding in, barking her head off. She jumps up on to my bed and begins slobbering all over my face. She's obviously been for her morning walk with Dad because she's covered in mud and gets it all over my duvet. It's hard to be mad though because she's so cute.

"Morning, Daisy." I laugh, trying to push her and her stinky breath away from my face. "All right, all right, I'm up."

"I'm afraid the twins have used up all the hot water again," Mum calls up the stairs. "Cold showers this morning!"

Roman slams open my door, making it bang against the wall. "Unlucky, loser!"

"Roman! I need to wash my hair this morning!" I groan, throwing my pillow at him, but he's already disappeared so it just plops on the floor. "You're so ANNOYING!"

"There is a little bit of hot water left," Reggie claims. "It wasn't completely ice cold when I got out."

"SHOTGUN!" John shouts from his bedroom.

"NO! I SHOTGUN!" I shout, jumping out of bed and racing towards the bathroom with Daisy jumping around my legs as I go, thinking we're playing some kind of game.

"**AHA!**" John grins, reaching the bathroom before me and shutting the door in my face. I hear the lock click.

"Nooooooo!" I bang on the door as the shower turns on. "Come on, John, I need to wash my hair."

"You snooze, you lose!" he calls back.

Grumbling about brothers, I plod back to my room with Daisy and climb into bed to wait for my turn. I pick up my book, deciding I might as well read while I wait. As I trace the title across the front cover with my

71

finger, I smile, still not quite believing what happened yesterday.

I met *Naomi Starr*. THE Naomi Starr.

OK, so I guess I didn't technically meet her but she was standing right there in the library with me for ages while she waited for her taxi. I wish I hadn't said that stupid thing about being her biggest fan – she must hear that all the time.

After she rushed out of there, I had stayed frozen to the spot and unable to speak for about five minutes. Rose found it hilarious and threatened to pour a bucket of cold water over my head to snap me out of it.

"That was Naomi Starr!" I finally managed to croak. "I can't believe it."

"I know. Not very nice in person, was she?"

"Naomi Starr. Standing right there," I gushed, ignoring her.

I didn't care that Naomi hadn't seemed that nice. I read online that she'd stormed out of her concert because she wasn't allowed a scheduled day off or something, so maybe she was just in a bad mood. Anyway, it didn't matter to me. *I had met Naomi Starr.*

"She took that book," Rose said all grumpily. "She didn't even say thank you."

"Maybe she'll return it," I said in a daze.

"I doubt it. Lucky for you, I have a second copy." She went into her office to find it and come back holding it out for me. "Don't lose it, Ruby, it's my last copy."

"Naomi Starr and I are borrowing the same book from the library!" I pointed out excitedly. "She'll be reading the same book as me!"

"Oh, Ruby," Rose chuckled, shaking her head at me, "I don't think she'll be reading that book any time soon. She was using it as a shield from the paparazzi. Anyway, I hope it helps you at least. Maybe you can learn to be confident just like that idol of yours."

"I hope so," I said gratefully, clutching **HOW TO SHINE**. "If she comes back to return the other copy, promise you'll let me know?"

She promised and then I came home, calling Beth as soon as I left the library to fill her in. She screamed down the phone for a LONG time.

It was much more satisfactory than the reactions from my family when I told them at home, which went as follows:

Dad: "Who?"

Mum: "What was that about books?"

Jeroame: "Is she the one in that girl band?"

Roman: "It would have been cooler to meet Riley Starr."

Reggie: "Remember that time I saw Elton John?"

John: "That wasn't Elton John. It was someone who looked a bit like him."

I phoned Isabella after dinner to tell her and she went, "Wow, that's SO cool, Rubes! What's she like? Uh-oh, I've got to go – we're off to a quiz night in the student union – but I'll call you tomorrow to hear about it, OK? Love ya, sis!"

At least someone in my family appreciated how big a deal it was, even if she couldn't hang around to talk about it.

It really was a big deal. The biggest deal. I'll never forget the moment I met Naomi Starr for as long as I live. I just *wish* I hadn't been so star-struck. Oh well.

I flick through **HOW TO SHINE** to get to the page I fell asleep on last night. It's a new chapter, titled: **STEP INTO SOMEONE ELSE'S SHOES**.

"I wish," I say out loud. "I'd do anything to be in someone else's shoes and not have to be in mine."

I don't know if it's because I'm still a bit overwhelmed with the excitement of yesterday, but as I begin to read through the chapter I feel a bit ... strange.

Everything starts tingling and I feel dizzy all of a sudden.

What's wrong with me?

CHAPTER EIGHT

NAOMI

Mum isn't speaking to me.

It's quite refreshing, actually. I should miss my concerts more often if it means I'm actually left alone for once in my life.

It's all over the news and I'm trending on social media. Apparently, storming out of your concert and leaving your fans waiting makes you a big diva and lots of people get very angry. I don't know why my publicity team are in such a state about it. My name is *everywhere*. Everyone is talking about me, even serious people on serious TV shows. I'm the most famous person in the world right now. You'd think my PR team would be having a party to celebrate this amazing brand opportunity.

But, noooooooo. Instead, they're whining about

having to work through the night and not getting any sleep or time off or whatever.

Now they know how I feel.

I've never seen Mum like she was when she got home last night. I did call her from our house when I got back to Chelsea and had access to a phone. I assured her I was safe and then said that even though I was still mad, I'd consider coming back to the arena to do the concert if she sent a car.

Apparently it was too late and by the time I got there and had my make-up and costumes sorted, the fans would have been waiting hours and we couldn't do that to them, especially as the arena shut at eleven and so on. **YAWN**.

She didn't even say sorry!

I thought that maybe, when she got home, she'd give me one of her classic lectures about how I shouldn't let people down, apologize for cancelling my day off, and then we'd go to bed and by the morning it would all be fine.

That's not what happened.

She got home looking REALLY bad. Like, no offence to her, but she really needs some time at a spa herself. An army of publicists had accompanied her home and they set up in my sitting room, pointedly talking loudly about the long night ahead of them.

"Remember to take off your shoes if you're going to be pacing," I'd reminded them.

Mum didn't even look at me. Without saying anything, she went to the fridge, got a bottle of water and just held it against her head.

"Mum," I began, following her into the kitchen, "I'm sorry that I didn't tell you where I was going, but I needed some space and I really think I deserve—"

She held up her hand to stop me.

"Please, Naomi," she whispered in this defeated, upset way which kind of shocked me. "Please, not now. I can't deal with it now."

And then she brushed past me and went into the sitting room to join the publicists, shutting the door firmly behind her, making it clear I wasn't welcome. I was a bit annoyed because if anyone should have been storming off and shutting themselves in a room, it was me.

Then, this morning, Simon knocked timidly on the door to announce it was time to get up.

"Where's Mum?" I yawned.

"She's downstairs. With everyone else," he said nervously.

"Can you tell her to come up here? We obviously need to talk about yesterday."

He hesitated. "Um . . . actually, she explicitly told me that she doesn't want to speak to you quite yet. I think she's got a lot on her plate and she's been working all night and she—"

"Whatever, Simon."

"Oh . . . sorry . . . it's Sam."

"Could you please ask Chef to make me another one of those green juices? I have a headache."

"Um . . . it's Chef's day off today."

I sighed irritably. "Then can YOU please make it? This headache is THE WORST!"

He nodded and scurried out of the room, shutting the door behind him, leaving me on my own to think over yesterday's events.

I get that people are angry. I really do. If I had bought a ticket to a concert and the singer hadn't shown up, I'd be annoyed too. But it's not like they won't get their money back. And I'm sure the crew at the arena have to put up with stuff like this all the time.

People online aren't saying very nice things about me. I try to stop myself from looking at my phone because I know it's not going to be good. But I don't realize quite how bad it is.

They don't get it, I tell myself, reading through the nasty comments and opinions. *They just don't understand.*

I turn off my phone and throw it across the room. I lie back on my pillows, not sure what to do. I don't want to go downstairs and face anyone yet. But I also know I won't be able to go back to sleep. I turn on to my side and see the book that I took from that library yesterday.

I reach for it and read the front cover: **HOW TO SHINE**.

I start turning through the first few pages to see what it's like. I have nothing better to do and maybe it will distract me from the nightmare that is my life.

I stop flicking the pages at a chapter title that catches my eye: **STEP INTO SOMEONE ELSE'S SHOES**.

"That's what everyone else needs to do," I mutter out loud. "Step into my shoes and see what it's REALLY like."

Maybe the mean online comments have affected me more than I thought because I start feeling a bit queasy as I read through the chapter.

"SIMON!" I yell. "WHERE'S THAT JUICE? I DON'T FEEL WELL."

My body goes all weird and tingly. I feel dizzy. Whoa. What's going on?

What's wrong with me?

CHAPTER NINE

RUBY

It happens when I get to a certain passage of the chapter. A lone paragraph in the middle of an otherwise empty page.

> *Sometimes, to learn about yourself, you need a different view. Step into someone else's shoes, tread in their footsteps, see things through their eyes.*
> *See how you shine.*

That's when I notice it. The book is ... wait, it can't be. Is the book ... *glowing*?

WHOOOOOOOOOOOOOOOSH!!

CHAPTER TEN

NAOMI

Wow, this book is seriously cheesy. This whole chapter is a bit of a yawn to be honest, but this bit on its own in the middle of the page looks like it might be mildly interesting.

> *Sometimes, to learn about yourself, you need a different view. Step into someone else's shoes, tread in their footsteps, see things through their eyes.*
> *See how you shine.*

OK, I really need Simon to get back here pronto with that juice because I think something's wrong with my brain. Is it just me or is the book ... *glowing*?
WHOOOOOOOOOOOOOOOOSH!!

CHAPTER ELEVEN

RUBY

(AS NAOMI)

For a moment, everything is dark.

I realize I must have fallen asleep and I sit bolt upright, blinking stupidly and panicking about how long I've been asleep for. My head aches but the dizziness has faded. The room comes into focus. I freeze.

Wait a minute. This isn't my room.

This room is **HUGE**. About five times the size of my bedroom. And it's *really* posh with a sparkling chandelier hanging from the ceiling, clean white walls decorated with expensive-looking art and tall windows with elegant grey velvet curtains. Dotted around the room are sleek vases filled with beautiful multi-coloured roses. I'm in a gigantic four poster bed with sheer fabric drapes and the softest silk sheets I've ever touched, and when I prop myself up, my hands sink into the mountain of squishy pillows behind me. The **HOW TO SHINE** book lies open on the page I was reading next to me.

Am I dreaming? I must be dreaming.

I shut my eyes tight. I open them again. No, I'm still here in this strange room. I pinch myself hard on the wrist but nothing happens.

"Is this ... heaven?" I croak, clutching the sheets in fear and looking around this perfect room. "Am I ... dead? I'M DEAD!"

"No, don't say that," someone replies by the door. "This will all blow over."

I yelp in surprise and a man comes hurrying over, carrying a silver tray with some glasses of green juice on it.

"Sorry! Sorry, I ... I didn't mean to frighten you! I did knock, I don't know if you heard." He holds out the tray. "Here! I made a few j-just in case. Sorry it took so long, I couldn't remember the exact recipe and I didn't want it to taste like pondweed so I took extra care."

I stare at him in horror.

"Are you all right?" he says after a few moments' silence. "You look ... upset."

"*Where am I?*" I whisper, barely able to speak.

"Sorry?"

"Where. Am. I."

His forehead creases in concern. "You're at home. In your bedroom."

"Is this some kind of joke? Some kind of prank? You look familiar. Did Roman and Reggie do this? Are you one of their friends? What's happening? Who are you?"

"I'm Sam, your assistant?" He gulps and picks up one of the juices, handing it to me. "I really think you should drink some of this. And I'll go get your mum. You don't seem . . . yourself."

He scurries out of the room, glancing over his shoulder with a worried expression as he goes. My heart is thudding so hard against my chest, I'm scared it will explode right out of there. This has to be some kind of dream but I've never had one so vivid, so real before.

I put the juice down on the bedside table and lift the silk duvet, sliding my legs out of bed. I realize I'm wearing the most beautiful pyjamas I've ever seen, and when I go to run my hand through my hair, I feel an eye mask resting on my head.

Who was that guy? I feel like I've seen him before but I can't think where. What did he say his name was? Was it Simon? No. Sam. Sam, an assistant, he said.

I click my fingers triumphantly. I know how I recognize him! He's Naomi Starr's personal assistant! I've seen him photographed trailing behind her before and I remember when she fired her last PA for selling stories about her to the press, social media went crazy about who would be next in line for the job. Apparently, Riley Starr, who was handling the process, received thousands of applicants. Beth had joked that I should apply.

I giggle, embarrassed that I'm so obsessed with Naomi Starr and her life that I'm apparently now dreaming about living it myself.

As nice as this dream is, I really should wake up. John has to be done in the shower by now and I don't want to be late for school. I pinch myself hard on the arm again.

The bedroom door opens and Sam comes in, but this time he's not alone. A tall, striking woman with amazing cheekbones glides across the room towards me wearing a long red kimono. **OH. MY. GOD.**

Riley Starr. It's Riley Starr! Naomi's mum! Walking towards me!

THIS IS THE BEST DREAM EVER!!

Without thinking, I jump to my feet and then, my brain frazzled with all this madness, I bow my head.

She stops and shares a look with Sam, who is wearing

the same baffled expression. She then folds her arms and sighs.

"What are you doing?" she asks, raising her eyebrows in a distinctly unimpressed manner.

"Sorry. That was stupid. Sorry. I don't know why I did that!" I laugh. "Hi, Riley Starr! It's you! Here in my dream!"

"What? What are you playing at?" She frowns. "Are you doing this for attention? What do you mean 'here in your dream'? You're not dreaming, you're wide awake as far as I can tell."

Something about her tone and the way she's looking at me makes the happy feeling I had about this whole dream thing start to fade away. She waits, tapping her foot impatiently, as I take a moment to scan the room. It's all very . . . real. Usually a dream is kind of blurry, right?

And are you ever this aware that you're in a dream? And if you are aware, isn't that when you usually wake up?

"Wake up," I say suddenly, closing my eyes and clenching my fists. "It's getting weird now. Wake up! Wake up!"

"I don't know whether you're playing up or whether you're hoping that all of this was some horrible dream, but let me assure you it's all too real," Riley Starr tells me tiredly. "We have been working through the night for you. We've released a statement on your behalf."

"I'm sorry, can I just—" I take some tentative steps towards her, my hand outstretched. "I need to check something."

My hand shaking slightly, I get closer to her and then poke her in the arm. I wait a second and then do it again, just to be sure.

"What on *earth* are you doing?"

"This is very weird. Very, very weird," I say, backing away from her, my throat closing up in panic. "B-because you seem real. Am I ... am I on a TV show? Have I won some kind of competition and blacked out from excitement and woken up in the middle of it all?"

Riley Starr and Sam stare at me.

"Because you're Riley Starr," I continue, pointing at her. "*The* Riley Starr. And I'm in this place." I gesture around the room. "This beautiful, amazing place." I bury my head in my hands. "*What is happening? I'm so confused!*"

"Look, I think that everything has got on top of you after last night—"

"The last thing I remember is reading the book," I say, trying to think logically and get my brain in focus. "I was reading the book and then I felt strange..."

"I cancelled your meeting for today," Riley says, looking pained. "I got the message loud and clear. And the record label is VERY angry, so it's probably a good idea to give it some time to blow over anyway. But what happened yesterday was completely unacceptable. You let thousands of people down."

"I-I let thousands of people down," I repeat slowly.

"I appreciate you owning up to it," she says, before taking a deep breath. "I also appreciate that this life is a hectic one. I never really had any days off when I launched my first few albums, but I also remember feeling overwhelmed at how chaotic my life was. So, with that in mind, I'm willing to put our discussion of yesterday's events on hold and have a day off with you. I want you feeling dedicated to your schedule, and if time off is the way to achieve that, then that's what we'll do."

I wonder if Riley Starr has lost her mind.

Then again, right now I'm wondering if I've lost *my* mind.

"Um. OK."

"I have organized a few things for you, just in case you want to go out and have some fun, but if you want to just sit home and relax, you can do that, too." She hesitates and then, as though convincing herself, says, "You've earned it."

"Would you like me to read the potential itinerary for the day?" Sam offers.

I assume he's asking Riley but they seem to both be looking at me for an answer.

"Sure?"

He begins to read aloud from a tablet.

"We have a massage and a manicure appointment booked in for you at home; there is a table reserved at the Ritz for brunch with Ms Starr later this morning; you've been invited to attend the premiere matinee performance of a new musical opening on the West End, the best seats in the house of course; then Westfield shopping centre in Shepherd's Bush has offered to close their doors to the public so you can shop for as long as you like this afternoon, everything you pick free of charge; and then this evening we have a selection of dinner reservations at London's top Michelin-starred restaurants, but if you don't wish to dine out twice in one day, we also have several chefs on call to cook whichever cuisine you would like at home. Oh, and I just got off the phone to Disney and they would love to provide an unreleased movie for you to watch in your home cinema this evening. They're going to send me some options."

My jaw drops to the floor.

"What do you think?" Riley Starr asks, examining

my expression. "Any of those take your fancy? You can pick and choose — there is no obligation. If you want to stay in bed all day and catch up on some much-needed rest—"

"ARE YOU KIDDING?" I start hopping up and down on the spot. "That all sounds AMAZING! I hope I never ever wake up from this unbelievable dream! Seriously, did I win a competition? Am I going to be on TV?"

There's a knock on the door and a woman pokes her head round.

"I'm so sorry to disturb, but the beauticians are here. Would you like them to start setting up for your treatments?"

Everyone turns to me again for an answer.

"YES, PLEASE! Wow, this is the best!"

Sam seems relieved.

"We'll see you downstairs when you're ready then," Riley says, turning to leave. "I have to do a bit more work and we'll head to brunch when your treatments are finished."

"Can I get you anything before I go?" Sam asks, following Riley to the door.

"No, I'm fine, thank you so much, Sam."

He gasps. "You . . . you called me Sam."

"Isn't that your name?"

"Yes," he whispers, a smile spreading across his face. "Yes, it is. *Thank you*."

"Oh, wait, Sam, do you know where the bathroom is?"

"The bathroom?"

"Yeah."

He looks at me as though it's a trick question, then says, "Your en suite is behind you, right through that door."

"I HAVE AN EN SUITE?"

I race excitedly towards the door he pointed out and open it to find the most beautiful bathroom I've ever seen in my life. It's floor-to-ceiling marble with a gold sink, a huge step-in shower and the biggest bath in the world.

I shut the door behind me and lock it.

"*What is going on?*" I whisper. "*What is happening?*"

Above the sink is a large, gold-framed mirror. I take a few deep breaths and then, swallowing the lump in my throat, I walk towards it, turning to look at my reflection.

"***AAAAAAAAAAAAAAAAAAAHHHHHHH
HHHHHHHHHHH!***"

CHAPTER TWELVE

NAOMI

(AS RUBY)

Something smells gross. Like dog's breath. Ew.

My vision is all blurry and I feel kind of dazed. I must have fallen asleep. I wonder what time it is. Why haven't I had my juice yet? What is taking Simon so LONG? He's lucky if I don't fire him. I blink the sleep out of my eyes.

My vision comes into focus and I realize there is a cold, wet nose touching mine.

A dog is panting right in my face.

"**AAAAAAAAAAHHHHHHHHHHHHHHHH!**"

I scream, jolting away from it and scrambling to get away, but the bed somehow disappears from beneath me and I fall off the side on to the floor. I get to my knees and carefully lift my head, peering over the side of the mattress. The dog is still there. It barks. I scream, ducking down.

"MUM! MUM! THERE'S A MANGY DOG IN THE HOUSE ATTACKING ME! GET IT OUT, GET IT OUT! CALL THE POLICE! SIMON! MUM! COME QUICK!"

The dog barks again and then jumps down off the bed and scampers out of the room. Breathing a sigh of relief, I get to my feet and look around.

"What the—"

I stumble backwards in shock and slam against the wall.

I'm not in my room. *I'm not in my room*! No wonder I fell off the bed so easily; this bed is the size of a small coffee table! And this bedroom is *tiny*! I don't think I've ever been in a room this small in my life! Am I in some kind of renovated cupboard?

Where am I? What's happening? Is this a nightmare?

"OK, this isn't funny. Wake up now, Naomi, wake up!"

I close my eyes and open them, but I'm still in this horrible cubby-hole. I try patting my cheek with the palm of my hand, but I don't seem to be able to wake up. I look down to see that I'm wearing flannel pyjamas with dogs all over them. I've never worn flannel pyjamas IN MY LIFE! As I clutch at my sleeve in horror at the pattern, I notice my nails. They're DISGUSTING. They're short and all the nail polish has been chipped! What's happened to my beautiful gel manicure that I had done at the spa the other day? WHAT KIND OF MONSTER WOULD DO THIS?

"I want to wake up now please!" I tell myself.

Nothing happens. And the worse thing is, it doesn't feel like a dream at all. Maybe I'm not asleep! Maybe this is real and I've somehow been brought here without my knowledge! Is this some kind of test? Has Mum decided to punish me for missing the concert last night and so has moved me in my sleep to a small bedroom/prison? That seems like an overreaction even by her standards.

"Mum? Are you there?"

No one answers. I don't think she would go this far to show how mad she is, would she? MAYBE I'VE BEEN KIDNAPPED. The last thing I remember is reading that stupid **HOW TO SHINE** book and then. . .

Wait. It's there on the bed. The **HOW TO SHINE** book! Open on the page I was reading. That's weird. Whoever kidnapped me must have taken the book, too.

It's a strange thing for a kidnapper to do, but whatever.

"OK, don't panic, don't panic," I repeat to myself, tiptoeing over to the door.

There are clothes strewn over the floor and books everywhere. I wrinkle my nose as I navigate the mess. I'm just thinking about how badly painted the blue walls are when I notice that one of them is covered in posters of . . . *me*.

Maybe it's a crazed fan who has kidnapped me!

"You are SO going to prison," I hiss at whoever's behind this.

The bedroom door is open a fraction from when that gross dog went out and I can hear a lot of noise coming from the rest of the house. I gulp, scared that there's more than one kidnapper. I see a tennis racket in the corner of the bedroom and I snatch it up, holding it at the ready. Peering through the door, I see the landing is empty and start to creep out silently.

There are voices downstairs but everyone seems to be talking over each other so I can't hear anything useful. There's a lot of clattering and what sounds like cutlery scraping on plates.

What is going on?

Suddenly, a door swings open and a teenage boy strolls out in a towel.

I scream, lunging forward and swinging the tennis racket with full force.

He dodges out of the way and then bursts out laughing as my enthusiastic swing sends me off balance and I go flying into the wall.

"Whoa," he says through his chuckling, "calm that rage! I wasn't *that* long in the shower and don't blame me for no hot water again. Blame Jeroame and the twins."

And with that he walks into another room and shuts the door, as though nothing out of the ordinary has occurred.

WHAT IS HAPPENING?!

I need to get to a phone immediately and call the police. And my driver. And Mum.

But before I can make any further progress, a woman appears on the stairs. She is wearing chequered pyjama bottoms and an oversized T-shirt that says "So Many Books, So Little Time" across the front. Her hair looks like it hasn't been brushed in weeks and she's carrying some pieces of paper with scribbles all over them.

"There you are!" she says, noticing me as I flatten myself against the wall, holding the tennis racket out in case she decides to attack. "Have you seen Daisy? Her paws are very muddy and I need to give her a bath before she ruins every bed in the house. I'm going to guess that she's already made herself at home on yours."

I blink at her.

"You had better get in the shower or else you're going to be late for school," she continues with a wave of her hand. "The boys are almost done with breakfast. It's not like you to be running this late. I suppose John got into the bathroom before you, did he?"

"If you don't let me go," I say as confidently as possible, every muscle in my body tense, "I will call the police!"

"What?" She smiles and puts her hands on her hips as though I've said something funny. "If I don't let you go where? Oh, it's not that school field trip that Roman and Reggie want to go on, is it? Look, darling, if you want to go then I will give my permission, but I don't think you'd enjoy rock climbing in Wales all that much."

"I will PERSONALLY call the Chief of Police and you will go to prison for the REST OF YOUR DAYS!"

"All right, all right, no need to be so dramatic!" she says, riffling through the pages in her hands. "You can go on the school trip if you like."

"WHO ARE YOU? WHAT DO YOU WANT WITH ME?"

"You haven't seen pages eighty-four and eighty-five anywhere, have you? I've left them somewhere and they're crucial to the plot," she says, ignoring me. "I'm meeting the author this morning. They're the next big thing; you heard it here first, Ruby."

"What sort of place is this?" I ask desperately, gesturing around me. "Where am I? Who is Ruby?"

"All important life questions, darling. I look forward to discussing those with you another time. Now, can you get ready for school, please!" she says, disappearing round the corner before I hear a door shut.

"This is crazy." I lower the tennis racket, bewildered. *"This is so weird."*

I hear the sound of paws plodding up the stairs and gasp when I see that big, fluffy, muddy dog appear on the top step. It spots me standing there and its tail starts wagging like mad, dirt splattering across the walls.

"Good dog!" I squeak, putting down the tennis racket on the floor so it knows I come in peace. "G-good dog!"

With an excited bark, it pelts towards me. I turn on my heel and run for my life, racing back into the bedroom and slamming the door behind me. The dog barks on the other side and then begins to whine noisily. After a few minutes, it gives up crying and instead I hear some weird slobbery noises.

Working out what to do next, I try to slow my breathing, but there's a loud knock on my door and I jump out of my skin.

"Ruby! You know how you attacked me with a tennis

racket when I came out of the shower? Did you mean to leave it on the floor out here?"

"Leave me alone!" I yell back.

"All right, calm down. I was going to let you know that Daisy has chewed up the grip. And broken quite a few of the strings. I'll take it downstairs and put it somewhere she can't reach. And hurry up, Ruby! If you miss the bus, Mum will make me stay behind with you and I need to get in early for the school paper editorial meeting."

"*Who is Ruby?*" I ask, tucking my hair behind my ear.

"RUBY!" Another voice yells through the door, making me jump away from it. "Hurry up! You've got five minutes before we go."

But as I touch my hair, I notice it's much knottier than normal. Like, SO much frizzier. Which makes no sense because I've been using this amazing, expensive conditioning mask recently to ensure this doesn't happen.

"First my nails and now my hair!" I exclaim, stomping my foot. "Who has done this to me?!"

There's a mirror in the corner next to the desk. My heart beating so hard that my ears are ringing, I kick aside the clothes and books on the floor and head towards it. And then I turn to see my reflection.

Oh. My. God.

My hands fly up to my face. It's not me! *My reflection isn't me*! It's that girl from the library!

I let out such a blood-curdling scream that three boys come bursting through the door and, before they can stop it, the dog slips through their legs and leaps at me with its giant muddy paws.

CHAPTER THIRTEEN

(AS NAOMI)

Who knew a limo had so many buttons?!

"Anyone would think you hadn't been in a limo before," Riley Starr says wearily, typing into her phone as I press the button that opens the door of a mini fridge in the armrest for the hundredth time.

It is so cool.

The whole limo thing is distracting me from the CRAZY that is my current situation. This is going to sound mad but, somehow, I have become *Naomi Starr*.

I KNOW.

None of this makes any sense! Obviously I've been freaking out about it ever since I first saw my reflection in the mirror an hour or so ago and there was Naomi Starr staring right back at me. I screamed so loudly that I fell backwards into the bath and then all these bodyguards came bursting into the room to check I wasn't being attacked by a crazed stalker or something.

"What's wrong?" one of them yelled.

"I'M NAOMI STARR!" I yelled back, scrambling out of the bath and pointing at my reflection in the mirror. **"I'M NAOMI STARR!"**

They were all silent and then they went away, one of them muttering, "Remind me never to work with pop stars again," as they left. I paced around the bathroom for ages after that, trying not to panic and wondering what I should do. I splashed cold water on my face several times, but every time I looked in the mirror, there was Naomi's face staring right back at me.

"How is this possible?" I whispered to no one.

I'm in Naomi Starr's body. And if I'm in her body, then what's happened to mine? And what's happened to Naomi?

I was freaking out. Freaking out **BIG TIME**.

After sitting on the bathroom floor for a few minutes trying to work out if I was crazy or not, Riley Starr knocked on the door asking if I was OK and did I still want the massage.

I thought about saying something along the lines of, "I actually don't have time for a massage right now because I have ended up in SOMEONE ELSE'S BODY."

But what was I going to do about it? I needed time to think and work out a plan. I needed to process the craziness of it all. I needed to stop freaking out and get my brain in gear. To do that, I needed to relax. . .

And what better way to relax than to have a massage?

If I was in Naomi Starr's body and everyone was treating me like Naomi Starr, then I might as well *act* like Naomi Starr, right?

And yeah, OK, so I haven't come up with a plan yet BUT I have had the best day of my life so far. The massage was incredible. They used all these amazing-smelling oils and stuff. I fell asleep within five minutes. Then, I was woken up half an hour later to have my nails done.

Sam kept bringing me healthy, delicious smoothies the whole morning and then he said, "Oh, Beyoncé has sent over her new album. Shall I put it on for you?"

"It's not out yet," I corrected him, enjoying my hand massage. "It's released in two weeks."

"Yes, but she's sent it to you ahead of release date," he replied. "As always."

I couldn't believe this was happening to me. ME.

Ruby! It didn't make any sense. I sat there, listening to incredible unreleased music, having my nails done and drinking freshly made smoothies when I should, in fact, be at SCHOOL.

Mwahahaha.

As someone named Tina massaged my temples in soothing circles whilst the last coat of polish was applied to my nails, I tried to work out exactly how this had happened. Was it all a crazy dream? Because, if not, and this was ACTUALLY happening, then it had to be down to some kind of. . .

Magic.

And that's stupid.

Anyway, I don't know what I'm going to do about it, but in the meantime, it is really fun to sit in a posh limo and press all the buttons on the way to brunch at the Ritz. Plus, I got to pick my outfit for the day from Naomi Starr's wardrobe. And let me tell you, she has A LOT of clothes. The wardrobe is basically the size of my house and is filled with every designer you can think of. Then, she has a separate wardrobe for shoes and handbags. Seriously. Her shoes have their OWN WARDROBE.

I decided on a blue Marina Blair dress to wear with tights and these amazing silver-studded black boots that I'd never be able to afford in a million years. It took me ages to pick a handbag, but I chose a leopard print one that I happen to know Naomi herself designed.

It went perfectly with the outfit and it was big enough to fit the **HOW TO SHINE** book in. It sounds weird, but I wanted to bring it with me because it was the last thing I remember reading as Ruby before this all happened. It felt important.

"By the way," Riley says, not looking up from her phone as we drive through central London, "it's going to be worse than usual when we get to brunch. Someone has leaked where we're going to the press."

"Don't worry, Ms Starr," the bodyguard sitting next to me replies. "It won't be a problem."

"Huh?" I say, noticing another button I haven't spotted before and pressing it. Blaring music suddenly fills the car.

"Naomi! Turn that down!"

"Sorry, sorry," I say quickly, pressing all the buttons to work out how to turn it off.

Luckily, Sam comes to my aid and leans over to press the right one and switch it off.

"As I was saying, it's going to be worse than usual," Riley warns me, although I have no clue what she's talking about. "As you can imagine, yesterday caused quite a stir. All of them will be here."

"All of who?"

"We're here," the driver says.

"Wait. Who's going to be here?"

No one answers me because they don't need to. As soon as the car door opens, there's an eruption of noise and hundreds of camera flashes as a huge crowd of paparazzi swarm around the limo.

Whoa.

"I've got you," the bodyguard says to me simply as I grip the edge of my seat. "Just keep your head down. The usual protocol."

"But—"

He climbs out of the car, shielding the doorway from the reporters desperately trying to reach over him with their cameras, lenses zooming in on me as I nervously slide across the back seat. I shield my eyes from the flashes and look for the sunglasses that Riley insisted I brought with me when I left the house.

"Let's go!" the bodyguard instructs impatiently.

I step out of the car and feel lost in a blur of noise and light. Someone's arm is gripping me tightly – the bodyguard's, I think – and another comes in to flank my other side. I'm dragged towards the door, barely able to see with all the cameras going off in my face, and tripping over my feet as the crowd surges to get closer to me. They're all shouting over one another, trying to get my attention by shoving microphones in my face.

"Naomi, what happened yesterday?"; "Naomi, why did you let down all your fans?"; "Is it true that you had a fight with your management and that's why you ditched the concert?"; "Naomi, who are you wearing?"; "Is it true you're retiring from music at the age of thirteen?"; "Do you have anything to say about the rumours that your record label is dropping you because of your diva behaviour?"; "Naomi, do you have a response to claims from your dancers that you never perform live?"

I'm pushed through the revolving doors and into a beautiful foyer. The noise of the reporters becomes muffled, drowned out by the soft tinkling of the piano being played in reception. I stop to catch my breath as the bodyguard lets go of my arm.

"That was horrible," I say, taking my sunglasses off. "I never want to do that again."

"Welcome back, Miss Starr," the head concierge says, coming over to greet me. "Would you like your usual table? We have it set up for you but can seat you somewhere else if you'd prefer."

"My usual table sounds great," I tell him, looking round me in awe. It's like a palace in here.

As we're shown to the best table in the restaurant, I start giggling.

"What's so funny?" Riley asks, as a waiter places her napkin on her lap.

"I feel so lucky. I can't believe I'm here at the Ritz. Having brunch with you." I take the gold-tasselled menu that a waiter is holding out for me. "This is all very surreal. It's amazing."

She looks taken aback. "I think that's the nicest thing you've said to me in a while."

I notice that guests at the other tables are staring at us. I suppose it's a bit odd that at the table next to us there's two uniformed bodyguards not eating and Sam scrolling through his computer tablet and every now and then picking up the phone and saying in a strained voice: "No, I'm afraid she is not available."

I catch the eye of a couple watching us from a table across the way. They quickly avert their eyes.

"Don't you ever get annoyed by it?"

"By what?" Riley answers, scanning the menu.

"Everyone looking at you all the time."

She pauses, thinking about her answer. "I've been in the public eye so long, I suppose I've grown used to it."

"Oh yeah." I nod. "Your first album came out when you were eighteen, right? And it was a huge hit right away."

"That's right. Feels like a long time ago." She smiles. "I still remember that feeling when my manager told me it had hit number one. It was incredible. My life was turned upside down."

"In what way?"

"Well" – she nods her head towards a table of people staring at us – "suddenly I was recognized everywhere I went. I wasn't born into this world, like you were. In one day, my life went from being completely unglamorous to being unbelievably wonderful. You can't imagine what that's like."

I smile to myself. "No, I can't possibly imagine."

"And that's why it's important to keep working hard," she says enthusiastically, leaning forward slightly, "why it's important to keep doing interviews and photo shoots and attending the right sort of events. I know it's tiring and can be boring, but, trust me, it's worth it. It's all crucial if you want to keep those albums going to number one and keep your career momentum." She waves her hand around. "All this can be taken away very quickly. It's about building a brand and we need to keep yours as strong as possible."

"But Naomi's brand ... I mean ... uh, *my* brand," I correct as she gives me a strange look, "as in, I mean, the Naomi Starr brand is pretty big."

"Yes, it is. Thanks to all the hard work you and your team have put in." She hesitates. "But if you do what you did yesterday every day – if you skip concerts and don't show up to rehearsals – then the fans will grow bored, the people you work with will grow bored, the media will grow bored and, eventually, the record label might grow bored. I've seen it happen to other pop stars. I don't want you to risk losing everything you've worked so hard to achieve."

"That makes sense," I say, smiling graciously up at the waiter placing a glass of sparkling elderflower in front of me.

"I'm saying all this, Naomi, because I want to explain why I've been so hard on you in rehearsals recently. And why I think it's a good thing that you're having a day off today to regather your strength and let your hair down. But tomorrow we need to get back to work – we need to fix everything that's happened and work hard to persuade the world it was a tiny glitch in your sparkling career. Does that sound like a plan?"

"Sure. It sounds like an excellent plan," I reply, imagining that's what Naomi would say.

She breaks into a smile, her shoulders visibly relaxing. "Great. I'm really glad we've talked about it. Now that we've got that out of the way, how do you feel about not talking about yesterday's nightmare for the rest of the day? Let's just concentrate on having some very welcome time off together. We don't get days like this very often, so let's make the most of it!"

"Yeah," I say with a wide grin, holding up my glass of elderflower to clink against her glass of champagne. "Let's."

CHAPTER FOURTEEN

NAOMI

(AS RUBY)

"Ruby! Wait up!"

A girl with bright pink hair, dressed in the same school uniform, is calling out to me as she comes up the road to the house I've just darted out from.

"You're going the wrong way to the bus stop," she points out. "Where are you going?"

"I need a car! Immediately!"

"Huh?"

"I said, I need a car! Do you have one?"

"Um, in case you've forgotten, we're thirteen years old so . . . no." She folds her arms, looking at me strangely. "What's going on?"

If only I could answer that question. I'm in some kind of horrific nightmare where I've landed in someone else's body. It sounds absolutely MAD, but it's true! When those three boys came bounding into the bedroom after I saw my reflection, I tried to explain to them what had happened.

"I'm Naomi Starr! NAOMI STARR!" I whimpered, looking at my reflection and seeing a stranger staring back at me. "I'm in someone else's body! **HELP ME!**"

They all started laughing at me and shaking their heads, one of them saying, "Whoa, Ruby, your obsession with that pop star has taken a new level." He then pointed at the uniform folded up on the chair by the desk and said, "You had better get dressed. We'll miss the bus."

When they left the room, I spent a few more moments freaking out before I got to action. I had to get out of that house and get back home, and I couldn't do that in pyjamas. The school uniform was better than nothing. I could see the **HOW TO SHINE** book lying on the bed as I got dressed into the disgusting uniform – seriously, forcing anyone to wear this horrible shirt is a CRIME – and decided to bring it with me. It's the only familiar thing to me right now.

I searched for something to carry the book in and all I found was an old, scruffy backpack.

"As if I'm going to be seen with this," I sighed, stuffing the book in there.

Then, before anyone could stop me, I raced down the stairs and out of the house, that scruffy dog barking as I left.

"I don't have time to explain but something . . . crazy has happened. I need a car to get to my house," I tell the girl with pink hair, desperately looking around to see where I am.

We're in a residential road and I don't see any taxis lurking nearby. I don't have any money but I can't worry about that. My mum will pay for everything once I get home.

"Your house is behind you," the girl says, pointing at the door I just sprinted from.

"Do you have a phone? Can you call me a taxi? It's an emergency."

"Why do you need a taxi? Should I be worried about you?" Her eyebrows furrow together. "Ruby, it's me! You can tell me anything!"

"Please just call me a car!" I demand impatiently.

"Not until you tell me what's going on," she says stubbornly. "You're not being yourself. If you're upset or worried about something, then I want to help."

UGH. You know, this is EXACTLY why I don't have friends.

They really hold things up.

"Fine." I let out a long sigh. "I am really Naomi Starr. I am trapped in this person's body. I need a car to get home so I can get back into my own body. I don't have a phone so I can't call one myself. I also don't know the numbers off by heart of my mum or my assistant. So I need you to call me a taxi to get me home to my Chelsea townhouse."

There's silence. Then, she starts laughing. Loudly.

"It's TRUE!" I insist, tapping my foot as she wipes away tears. "Now, can you call me a taxi? You said you wanted to help."

"I have to say," she says through giggles, "I considered trying to get out of the maths test today, too, but **WOW**, you have come up with the most imaginative excuse EVER."

Realizing that she's never going to believe the truth, I decide it's probably best to come up with another tactic.

"OK, I'm this Ruby person and I'm trying to get out of school, you caught me," I say, holding up my hands. "Will you help?"

She stops laughing and her eyes widen. "Are you serious? You actually want to skip school today?"

"Yes!"

"You've NEVER done that. What's going on? Is this because of what happened on the bus yesterday with Ali inviting John to her party and not you?"

"Yes." I nod gravely, playing my part outstandingly, I must admit. Maybe I should consider branching into acting once I've sorted out this mess. "Yes, that is why. I love John and it is too painful seeing him with Ali."

The girl wrinkles her nose. "Did you just say you love John? As in your *brother*, John?"

Damn it.

"I mean, I love my brother John because he's my brother. And . . . and I don't want him to go to Ali's party. Obviously. Because Ali is" – I take a stab in the dark – "not nice?"

For a moment, I think I've messed up everything, but then the girl starts nodding in understanding. **PHEWF**.

"Yeah. I suppose it would suck if John started hanging out with people like Ali. But I don't think you need to worry; he's two years older than her. She only invited him and his friends to try to look cool in front of Noah." She hesitates. "You're really *that* upset about it?"

"Yes. I am. I don't want to face Alice."

"Ali," she corrects, confused.

"You see? Just saying her name is too painful. And I don't want to talk about it any more. I also want a taxi. Please help me. *As my friend.*"

"Where are you going to go?" she asks, looking concerned. "Can't you just hang around the library or something?"

"Yes. That's where I'll go. The library. So, you don't need to worry."

"You can walk to the library. You don't need a taxi."

"I want to go to another library. A big one far away," I say, getting irritated. Who is this person and why is she asking a BILLION questions?

"The British Library?"

"YES! Sure. The British Library. There's a . . . uh . . . book there. It's the only thing that can comfort me right now."

"That sounds like you," she says, giving a small smile. She glances back towards the front door of Ruby's house. "All right. We better move fast though before your brothers come out to get to the bus. Let's get to the main road and if there's no taxis, we can google a cab company."

"THANK YOU!" I say, feeling like I could hug her.

Which is strange. I very rarely feel like hugging anyone. Because, you know. Gross.

I follow her lead as she heads in the opposite direction I was going, following the pavement round until it reaches a busier road. There are a few students in the same uniform as us gathered around the bus stop nearby.

"Come on," the girl says, ushering me away from

them and ducking behind a corner shop. "I don't think you'll get a taxi, so I'll call you one. What happened to your phone by the way?"

"Uh ... the dog ate it," I say, as she googles a company and rings them.

"OK, the taxi is on its way," she tells me, hanging up. "I better run for the bus. Are you sure you're all right?"

"Yes, I am. Thank you so much ... uh ... you. And don't worry. I'll be back to normal in no time."

She nods, not looking like she quite believes me, and then says goodbye, going to join the students waiting for the bus. When the taxi pulls up, I hop in and give the driver my townhouse address, feeling a little bit better. At least I'm on my own now and can freak out in peace.

How did this happen? How did I end up in someone else's body?

Wait – does this mean that Ruby is in my body? In my house? With **MY** things? **LIVING MY LIFE?**

Oh my God.

If she even THINKS about touching my clothes, she's in SERIOUS trouble.

And don't get me started on my shoes.

"Here we are," the driver says cheerily, as we finally pull up at the house. "Do you want to pay cash or card?"

"I will send someone to pay you," I say, before jumping

out and running towards the gates of my house.

"**HEY!**" he yells after me, getting out of the car. "**OI! COME BACK HERE!**"

"Wait one moment!" I call back as politely as I can muster. "I will have one of my staff pay you."

He mutters something under his breath and then waits, leaning back on his car and watching me like a hawk. I press the buzzer on the gates. It rings and then a voice comes crackling through the intercom.

"Hello?"

"HI! Hi, hello!" I say excitedly, forgetting about the whole body swap thing for a moment and waving at the camera. "Can you let me in? It's Naomi!"

"Naomi who?"

"Naomi Starr!"

There's silence before the voice says, "Please leave the property immediately, thank you."

"No! No wait! It's me! I'm just in someone else's body!"

"I'm asking you politely and calmly to leave the premises. Thank you."

WHY WILL NO ONE BELIEVE ME?!

Although . . . *would I believe me*? Probably not.

If I'm in this Ruby person's body, there is a high chance she might be in mine. And she may be as freaked out and confused as I am. I HAVE to speak to her. I can't give up.

"I have an appointment with Naomi Starr," I say, after I've pressed the buzzer again. "Is she in? Look, could you just ask her? Please, say a girl named *Ruby* is asking for her. I bet she'll let me in if you tell her that."

"Please leave the premises before we call the police," the voice says snappily. "**NOW**."

HOW DARE THEY SPEAK TO ME LIKE THAT?!

"When I get back in my body, you are SO FIRED!" I yell into the speaker.

My threat is greeted with silence. I press the buzzer again and again but there's no response. Refusing to take no for an answer, I consider climbing the gate. I mean, how hard can it be? People do it in films all the time.

I march up to the gate confidently and place my hands on the bars, attempting to hoist myself up. I try to find a grip with my feet but my shoes keep slipping. I can't get anywhere near the top of the gates, let alone over them. I decide a run up might be helpful, that way I can kind of leap upwards and get a head start. But I don't get any further from the ground. After some attempts, I become conscious of the giggling behind me.

I turn to see the taxi driver laughing his head off.

"Excuse me, but what's so funny?"

"You trying to climb the gate," he replies bluntly, getting his phone out. "I need to film this."

"If you do, I shall add you to my list of people I'm going to sue! The person who answered that buzzer is one of them and you are next on the list."

"Hey, you owe me the taxi fare," he argues, frowning. "So, I'm the one who will be suing YOU."

"I would be able to pay you the fare if they'd let me talk to Riley or Naomi Starr!" I cry, gesturing at the gates. "I'm not making this up. If I was trying to get out of the fare, wouldn't I have run away by now? I promise I know Riley Starr and she will pay you as soon as I explain everything."

He sighs heavily. "OK, say you're telling the truth. Why don't you just look on social media?"

"Look on social media for what?"

"For where they are. Here." He types something into his phone, waits a moment and then starts scrolling down his screen until his face suddenly lights up. "There! Found them. They're going for brunch at the Ritz."

"How do you know that?"

"Because it's all over Twitter, see? I searched for Naomi and Riley Starr. People have posted photos of them heading in. They must have just left before we got here."

"THEN WHAT ARE WE WAITING FOR? Quick!"

I fling open the door to the backseat. "We need to get there! Go, go, go!"

He reluctantly gets in and, after a firm promise from me that he will DEFINITELY be paid for both journeys, we set off into central London. I feel a sense of renewed hope now that we've managed to track them down and leap out of the car as soon as we pull up to the front of the hotel.

"You're not getting away that easy," the taxi driver says, following me in.

I'm through the revolving doors so fast that by the time the doormen open their mouths to ask if they can help with anything, I'm already halfway down the gallery to the restaurant, the driver hot on my heels.

I march into the restaurant, scanning round the room until I spot them. And when I do my heart skips and I feel like I might faint.

Because it's really quite weird to see my mum on the other side of the room clinking her glass with ... well ... *me*.

CHAPTER FIFTEEN

RUBY

(AS NAOMI)

I drop my glass.

The sparkling elderflower spills all over the table and splashes Riley Starr's dress, but I don't care. Because I'm watching an angry-looking man come striding over towards a table behind ... *me*.

"Hey!" she says, sounding VERY angry. "Get out of my body!"

I can only stare at her. Because it's me. ME! Standing right there!

This is so *weird*.

"Oh my goodness, Miss Starr, Ms Starr, I'm so sorry," one of the waiters is saying, as several staff come hurrying over to usher her away from the table. "Please follow me out of the restaurant and leave the Starrs to their brunch."

"I will **NOT** leave them to their brunch," the-Ruby-who-isn't-me says, swatting his hand away, "because **I AM A STARR!** Mum! It's me!"

Oh my god. Naomi Starr is in my body. **NAOMI STARR IS ME.**

"I've never seen this girl in my life," Riley says, horrified at what's going on.

"Someone owes me a taxi fare!" the angry man is saying, pointing to Riley. "Apparently, *you're* going to pay it!"

"I don't know how you got in here," the head waiter says through gritted teeth to them. "But please kindly leave—"

"SHE'S IN MY BODY! TELL HER TO GIVE IT BACK!"

"Wait!" I jump to my feet. "It's OK, you don't need to send them out. Uh ... *Ruby*, why don't we go speak in private?"

"You know this girl?" Riley asks, stunned.

"Yes," I squeak, my mouth dry. "She's an old friend."

"An old friend from where? I didn't realize you had any old friends."

"Oh, well, you know me. I'm very ... secretive about

124

these things. Anyway, I'll be back in one second," I inform her, picking up my handbag and gesturing towards the door. "We have something important to talk about."

"I demand to be paid!" the taxi driver practically yells.

"I don't have any money," she seethes. "Maybe, *Naomi*" – if looks could kill, I'd be dead right now – "you could kindly ask your *mum* to help out."

I clear my throat. "Yes. Yes, Mum, would you mind paying this man the taxi fare? I'll pay you back, I promise. Sorry."

"All right," she says wearily. "I'll sort out the fare. But then you come back and tell me what this is all about please, Naomi."

"Of course. Thanks so much. You're the best mum ever."

Naomi snorts, following me out of the restaurant as we leave Riley to sort things out. "I would never say something lame like that."

"Excuse me, is there somewhere private I could have a conversation with my friend?" I ask a waiter at the door to the restaurant.

"Of course," he says warmly, directing us into a small dining room off the main gallery.

As soon as the door shuts and we're alone, she explodes.

"OK, WHAT is going on? Did you do this? Did you

steal my body? WHO ARE YOU?! Change us back! **CHANGE US BACK NOW!**"

I hold up my hands, backing away from her. "I'm as freaked out as you are! I have no idea what's going on, I swear!"

"You've stolen my body!"

"You've stolen mine!"

"WHY WOULD I STEAL SOMEONE'S BODY?"

"I don't know! I don't know how this has happened. . ." I hesitate as something dawns on me. "Wow! I'm talking to Naomi Starr!"

"YES!" she says, exasperated.

"Oh my God. Sorry, it just hit me that I'm actually meeting you. I can't believe I'm meeting Naomi Starr. I'm a **HUGE** fan. And you're me right now! That's mad. Naomi Starr is me and I'm Naomi Starr. Whoa." I run a hand through my hair. "This is so crazy."

She stares at me. "You mean, you're not behind this? You didn't do this body swap thing on purpose?"

"Of course not! And I know that this is weird circumstances, but can I just say something to you. . ." I take a deep breath. "You are my favourite pop star ever, in the whole world. I think you're amazing and I love all of your songs. It's a real honour to meet you. I'm seriously star-struck."

She doesn't look impressed. "Whatever. Did you, or did you not, perform some kind of magic spell to switch with me and steal my life?"

"NO! I have no idea what's going on. I woke up as you. And I have been freaking out all morning."

She narrows her eyes at me. "How did this happen? You were in the library yesterday, right? That was you."

"Yes, that was me."

"So maybe something happened to us then? Maybe we both walked through body-morphing nuclear waste on our way into the library or something? That's the sort of thing that happens in films."

I can't help but laugh. She glares at me.

"Have you got a better explanation?" she asks, folding her arms.

"No, sorry," I say hurriedly, my cheeks burning. "I don't remember any ... uh ... nuclear waste though. Surely we would have noticed walking through it?"

"Then what could it be?" she wails, beginning to pace around the room. "We have to switch back! This is insane! I don't want to wake up again with a stinky dog slobbering over my face!"

"You met Daisy!" I exclaim, excited that Naomi Starr has met my dog. "She's super friendly. Did you meet any of my family? Your mum is really cool and your assistant is so nice. I really—"

"I don't care what you think of Simon!" she snaps.

"Sam," I correct quietly, but then wish I hadn't said anything because her hands clench into fists.

It's strange seeing me so angry. I had no idea that's what my face looks like when I'm cross. My eyeballs kind of stick out and my mouth goes very small, until it almost disappears.

"We need to fix this," she says through gritted teeth.

"Let's go from the beginning," I suggest, desperate to be helpful. I sit down at the table and gesture for her to follow suit. "What's the last thing you remember as Naomi?"

"I was in bed. Simon was getting me a juice. I was reading. Then, the next thing I remember is waking up as you, feeling very dazed. It was like my brain was all foggy."

"That's exactly the same for me. The last thing I remember is reading and then I woke up in your bed."

She frowns in concentration. "What were you reading?"

"That book from the library, **HOW TO SHINE**."

She gets to her feet so fast, her chair is knocked backwards. She holds up my backpack and pulls out a copy of **HOW TO SHINE**, slamming it on the table.

"That's what I was reading, too!" she exclaims, pointing at it. "That's it! That has to be it! We were both reading the same book and then **BAM!** It swaps us. I remember it glowing."

I open her handbag and pull out my copy, placing it on the table next to hers. "You really think these books switched us?"

"What else could it be? And, look, we've both brought our copies with us. That's got to mean something! We're connected to these books somehow," she says excitedly, flicking through her copy until she stops at a specific page. "This is where I got to. This is the last thing I remember reading."

Sometimes, to learn about yourself, you need a different view. Step into someone else's shoes, tread in their footsteps, see things through their eyes.
See how you shine.

"SAME!" I gasp, flicking to the page in my copy.

"Maybe that will swap us back! We just read the passage at the same time and that's that." She claps her hands making me jump. "Problem solved."

"You think it will work?"

"One way to try. We have to read it at the exact same time. On the count of three."

"Are we reading it out loud?"

She looks thoughtful for a moment. "No. The first time I wasn't reading it out loud. Were you?"

I shake my head.

"Let's try reading it in our heads first and if that doesn't work, we'll read it out loud at the same time. Ready?"

I pull the book towards me in preparation. She takes a deep breath and I notice her crossing her fingers.

"One ... two ... three!"

I read through the passage. Nothing happens. I read through it again from the top, just to be sure. But I'm still Naomi.

"It didn't work!" she yells.

I realize that I would have been disappointed if it had. I've spent hours lost in daydreams about what it's like to be Naomi Starr. About how amazing it must be to have no problems at all; to be so famous that you get freebies wherever you go and people act crazy when you walk into a room. I've wondered what it feels like to be so talented at something, that you know exactly where you belong and where your life is going.

I've only been Naomi Starr for a few hours and it's been everything I dreamed of. No one has spoken over me or walked into me and pretended I don't exist. I haven't had to worry about going to school and sitting through boring lessons I don't understand. No one has purposefully reminded me that I'm excluded from a party because I'm not cool or interesting enough to be there.

And best of all, no one has thrown mashed potato at my head.

"Let's try reading it out loud," she instructs, picking up her copy of the book.

But that doesn't work either. We read it out loud together three times, just in case.

"**ARGH!** Why isn't this working?" she yells, throwing the book across the room and then sitting down in a strop.

It's very odd to watch myself acting that way. If the situation wasn't so serious, I'd be laughing at how much of a diva it looked like I was being. If I ever tried to behave this way at home, my brothers would find it hilarious, make fun of me and then play some kind of prank to put me back in my place, like throwing a bucket of ice water over my head while I slept.

Come to think of it, maybe it is a good idea to swap back. She is **NEVER** going to survive in my house.

"Hang on," I say, running my finger across the sentences we've been reading. "Maybe it's not a case of reading the passage. Maybe it's about *listening* to it."

She blinks at me. "Like, get an audio version?"

"No, listen to what the passage is saying. It's about seeing things through someone else's eyes, right?" I read it out loud again slowly, so we can really take in the words. "*Sometimes, to learn about yourself, you need a different view. Step into someone else's shoes, tread in their footsteps, see things through their eyes. See how you shine.*"

"The book wants us to see things from each other's point of view?" She looks at me in disbelief. "But whyyyyyy? I'm very happy seeing things from MY point of view!"

"It's saying that we'll learn something about ourselves by being in each other's shoes." I take a deep breath. "I think we have to go along with it. Maybe that's the way to swap back."

"Are you serious? The way to swap back is for me to live your life? How can I possibly be expected to do that? I can't live in that house! Sleep in that bedroom! Your brothers are so loud. Your dog is so smelly. And seriously, what is with the flannel pyjamas, Ruby? FLANNEL. This can't be happening to me! I can't go to school! I've never been to school before – I don't even know what to do at a school! I'm NAOMI STARR. I can't be around . . . *normal people!*" She hesitates, before adding, "No offence."

"None taken."

And I mean that. I've seen how Naomi lives her life and this is definitely going to be a challenge for her. She paces around a bit more lost in thought and then eventually stops, leaning back against the wall and closing her eyes.

"I guess it's the only thing we can do. No one will believe that this has happened. If we tell anyone, they'll think we're crazy," she admits, looking crushed. "How long do you think it will take? Are we talking hours? Days? **MONTHS?**"

"I don't know. But we'll swap numbers, use each other's phones and keep in touch. We can send updates and help each other out. Give tips on how to be . . . us. I know it's going to be strange for you going to school, but if you could go along with it and not get me expelled that would be great."

"I think I met one of your school friends earlier," she remembers. "Someone with pink hair."

"Beth!" I grin, thinking about how Beth would react if she ever found out that I'd lived a day as Naomi Starr. "She's my best friend! She's great, you're going to love her. Which friends of yours should I know about?"

Her eyes drop to the floor and she mumbles, "None."

"Oh. OK." *She doesn't have* **ANY** *friends?*

133

"Do you really think this will work?" she asks, changing the subject. "You really think if I pretend to be you and you pretend to be me, suddenly we'll just magically switch back?"

"I think it's worth a try," I say confidently. "And maybe it will be fun! It's like stepping into a virtual reality or something."

She rolls her eyes. "Sure. Whatever. We had better get on with it. The sooner we do this, the sooner we'll switch back. And make sure you keep me updated every day. I'm guessing your phone is somewhere in your room?"

"Yeah, on my desk, usually under a book. I'll text my number from your phone right now. I found it on the floor before I left."

"I threw it across the room when I read some mean things about me online," she explains, before glaring at me. "Try not to make my reputation any worse than it is right now. I have a career and I don't want that to be ruined for ever."

"Don't worry, your mum already gave me a lecture about that. I promise I won't ruin anything."

I can't believe this is happening. This is ACTUALLY happening.

It feels like I'm in a dream. I get to be Naomi Starr! **NAOMI STARR!** I get to be a famous pop star with no troubles and a life of luxury. This is like the craziest, most amazing dream EVER! I'm so happy and excited, I'm scared that I'll BURST.

I have to make the most of Every. Single. Moment.

"I hope for your sake that we've swapped back by tomorrow night," she says glumly, going to open the door.

"Why?"

"Because of the concert."

"What concert?"

"Didn't Mum tell you? I'm supposed to be performing in Berlin to seventeen thousand people." She offers me a small smile. "I already skipped out on one concert this week; there's no way they'll let me get out of another."

And just like that, the happy feeling vanishes.

CHAPTER SIXTEEN

NAOMI

(AS RUBY)

"I can do this," I say out loud, gazing up at the building in front of me. "It's just school. I've seen schools in movies. It's not a big deal."

I head up the concrete steps and push open the door, stepping into a long, empty corridor. It has a lot of truly terrible artwork up on the walls and it smells funny. No wonder people hate school if it smells this bad. The strip lights along the ceiling are also weirdly bright. Are they trying to blind their students?

Before I left Ruby at the Ritz, she told me that I'd have missed most of the morning's lessons by the time I got here so to head to the school library and wait there until lunch. Apparently, all I had to do was find Beth and stick with her. We have all our classes together.

I walk towards the double doors at the end of the corridor, as Ruby instructed me to do, and let out a long sigh.

As IF I am at school right now. Me. Naomi Starr. In a *school*.

This whole situation is so wrong it makes me want to puke down this gross uniform.

"Ruby! There you are!"

I jump as a voice bellows down the corridor. One of the doors I just sauntered past has swung open and a scrawny, dark-haired man with glasses and a thunderous expression has stuck his head out of it. He has a weirdly small head and scrunched-up features. He reminds me of an angry ferret.

"Where have you been?" he asks, coming to stand in the doorway. "And where exactly are you going?"

I am not prepared for this ambush.

"Uh, where do *you* think I am going?" I ask, hoping he'll give me the correct answer to his question.

"I have no idea, but I know where you should be! In my lesson! Do you have a reason as to why you've missed a morning of classes?"

"Yeah," I shrug, remembering what Ruby told me to

say. "I had a doctor's appointment. Didn't my parents tell you? They rang reception this morning."

He frowns. "I didn't get the message."

He shoots me a suspicious look but then steps back, gesturing into the classroom. "Come on then, sit down. You can catch up on what you missed later, including the test at the start of the lesson."

I guess Ruby was right about the doctor's appointment excuse working.

"Don't worry, they'll believe you," she'd said confidently, leaning on the reception of the Ritz as the concierge sorted a prepaid taxi to get me to the school. "I've never been in trouble before so they won't suspect anything. And frankly, I'll be surprised if anyone even notices I haven't been there all morning."

It wasn't part of the plan to go straight into lessons, but I don't really have much of a choice. The angry-ferret teacher is staring me down.

"Cool," I say, striding into the lesson. OK, so I wasn't prepared for this, but it's not like I can't handle it.

Please. I'm Naomi Starr. I can handle anything.

"Where shall I sit?" I ask him.

"In your normal seat," he replies grumpily, closing the door and going to his desk at the front.

Luckily, there's only one spare seat in the classroom

so I'm guessing that's mine. It's in the middle towards the back. I take in my fellow classmates, most of whom haven't even bothered to look up from their books at my arrival. This is highly unusual for me. Normally, when I walk into a room, everyone pays attention.

I know I'm technically Ruby right now, but still. It's irritating.

That girl with pink hair, Beth, is sitting at a table by the window and sits up straight when I walk in, giving me a wave. I acknowledge her with a nod.

"OK, where were we?" the teacher says in a tired voice, turning to the white board behind him, which has loads of equations on it.

Ugh. This must be a maths lesson.

The teacher, whose name I discover is Mr Jones, starts droning on about something boring and I take the opportunity to have a good look at my surroundings. That's what the stupid book wants me to do, right? See things from Ruby's point of view or whatever, and then I can learn something about myself and transfer back to my life.

OK, so through Ruby's eyes I can see the following: a lot of bored students are pretending to listen; the boy next to me is doodling in his textbook; the girl next to him clearly hasn't brushed her hair in a couple of days;

the girl in front of her is texting underneath the desk; and a boy on the other side of the room is flicking ink at the people in front of him.

What can I learn about myself from this? I don't suit a school atmosphere.

Great! I feel totally enlightened. I close my eyes and hope that's enough to land me back in my body.

"Ruby, am I disturbing you from your nap?"

I open my eyes to see Mr Jones glaring at me.

"No, don't worry about it," I reply graciously. "Carry on with ... whatever you were talking about."

His beady, ferret eyes go all wide, like they might pop out of his head. Some of the other kids in the class swivel in their seats to look at me with confused expressions.

"How kind of you. I don't know what's wrong with you today, Ruby, but please refrain from closing your eyes and instead pay attention in my class," Mr Jones replies through gritted teeth, before pointing at the board. "Now, how about you come up here and solve this equation for everyone?"

"No thanks, maths isn't my thing."

This prompts a ripple of giggles and even more baffled expressions. I wonder if Ruby is really good at maths and that's why my reply has had such an effect.

"I see," Mr Jones says, bristling. "Perhaps detention is your thing?"

I snort. "I don't think so. Pretty stupid thing to say. No one likes detention, right?"

"That's it. You've landed yourself detention for this evening."

"Are you serious? For what?"

"For an appalling attitude!" Mr Jones claims. "I don't know what has got into you!"

"Just because I didn't come up to the front of class and solve an equation, I get detention? That's SO unfair!" I turn to the boy sitting next to me. "Is he always like this? Because if so, you guys should really sue. I can recommend an *excellent* lawyer."

"RUBY!" Mr Jones cries, his face a dangerous shade of red. "How dare you speak to me like this!"

"I wasn't speaking to you; I was talking to this person." I jerk my head at the boy sitting next to me, before shooting Mr Jones a warning look. "And if I were you, I'd be seriously careful about your tone because I wasn't lying. My lawyer is the best in the country."

There's a collective gasp from the other students, before they burst into giggles, enjoying the drama. I don't really get what the big deal is. Hello, if someone is going to be rude to me, then I will be rude back. No one tells me what to do.

Mr Jones looks as though he might explode with anger. He points a finger at the door.

"Get. Out. Of. My. Class," he wheezes. "NOW."

"Perfect!" I jump to my feet, grabbing my bag. "Yeah, this wasn't really working for me. Can someone point me in the direction of, like, a relaxation room? I'm guessing you don't have spa facilities here, but maybe there's a lounge or something where I can get some coffee?"

They stare silently at me. Mr Jones's jaw is on the floor.

Wow. These people are so rude.

"OK, whatever, thanks for the help," I mutter under my breath, marching out of there and closing the door behind me with a slam.

There are no signs anywhere, which is super annoying, so I make the decision to go to the library until lunch. I'm guessing it will be quiet there, so at least no one will bother me and I can ask that Beth person where the lounge is later.

The library is empty, so I sit in one of its very uncomfortable chairs and wait for lunchtime.

YAWN. This is so boring. I slide down into the seat and WISH I at least had Ruby's phone on me to go on social media or something. My experience of school so far hasn't exactly gone well. Who does that Mr Jones think he is? I can't believe Ruby puts up with him. And how long are students expected to sit in lessons for? I was only in there for a maximum of ten minutes and that was enough, thank you very much.

Suddenly, a horrible bell rings out loudly. I can hear commotion in the corridor outside the library as kids spill out of their classrooms.

THANK GOODNESS. Lunchtime. I hope they have good restaurants in this place because I'm famished.

"Ruby! I thought you might be hiding in here."

Beth comes over, drops her bag on the table and then puts her hands on her hips.

"What WAS that?" she asks.

"What?"

"Oh, I don't know, maybe your showdown with Mr Jones? That was crazy!"

"It's not a big deal. He's SO annoying. Also, don't you think he looks like an angry ferret?"

"You're going to be in a lot of trouble. I saw him marching towards the headmaster's office after class."

"So?"

"So, this is really unlike you," she says slowly, as though I'm not getting something. "Ruby, you're acting strange today. Is everything OK? Did you find that book you were looking for at the British Library?"

"Huh?" Then I remember our conversation this morning when she helped me get a taxi. "Oh, yeah. I did. So, shall we go have lunch?"

She nods, a smile creeping across her face. "OK. Are you sure everything's all right? I've never seen you like this before."

"Like what?" I ask, following her out of the library and into the chaos of the corridor.

Ew. There are people **EVERYWHERE**.

"I don't know. You're just ... different. You're even walking differently. It's like you're much more sure of yourself."

"What kind of food do they serve here?" I ask, bored of the conversation. "Do they have a selection of restaurants or just the one? Because I have a few dietary requirements that I'll need to inform the chef."

Her stunned expression reminds me that I'm meant to be Ruby and she would know how many restaurants there are because she goes to school here all the time.

"I mean ... what do you feel like eating today?" I say quickly, hoping that covers my mistake nicely.

"Whatever the vegetarian dish is, like we always get," she replies, still watching me suspiciously.

Pretending to know exactly where we're going, I

follow her round a corner and down another corridor, towards a set of bright green doors.

Who decided on the interior design of this place? They should be fired.

Beth swings open the door and I'm hit by a wave of noise. I gasp in horror at the sight before me as I step into the room. It's not a restaurant at all, but some kind of *canteen*. There are kids everywhere and they're all talking over each other, laughing loudly and showing each other things on their phones, while cutlery scrapes and clatters on plates.

Worse than that, there isn't table service! I don't see one waiter, not one. Instead, we're expected to pick up a gross, damp tray – a TRAY – and queue up to get our food from a bizarre buffet-type serving area.

"You are joking, right?" I blurt out, disgusted as Beth passes me a tray.

"This tray's not too wet," she insists, holding it out for me. "The one below it is worse. I've checked."

I take it reluctantly, holding it at arm's length.

"**EUGH**, it smells so GROSS in here!" I retch as we join the back of the queue. "I am not eating anything served here."

"It doesn't look too bad," she says, craning her neck to see over the people in front of us.

"Is this the only place to get food around here? I am SO ordering in. There's got to be a good restaurant around here somewhere that delivers. Can I borrow your phone?"

She bursts out laughing. "You're being so weird today!"

Not to be rude, but she didn't exactly answer my question. I'm about to tap her on the shoulder and ask again when some girl with long, glossy red hair comes marching over to us as though she owns the place.

"Hi, Ruby," she says crossly, putting her hands on her hips. Another girl has accompanied her and seems to be copying her every move, including the hands on hips pose.

Beth rolls her eyes at me. I take a wild guess that this is someone neither of us like.

"So, I spoke to John," the girl says, all narky.

"OK," I reply, already bored. "Good for you."

"He told me you never gave him the invitation."

"What invitation?"

She looks at me as though I've just slapped her across the face.

"The invitation to my party! The one I gave you on the bus yesterday? I told you to give it to him!"

"Give out your own invitations," I say, looking her up

146

and down because NO ONE talks to me this way. "Who do you think you are?"

My words have an immediate effect. I hear a sharp intake of breath from Beth next to me, while everyone in the queue around us is staring and whispering. The canteen starts to descend into a hush as people become interested in our conversation.

From the way this girl is acting, I take it that she is one of those popular kids I've seen in movies, who everyone worships, but is also scared of.

And from how surprised everyone is that Ruby is standing up to her, I guess that Ruby is the opposite.

Oh well. Time for a change.

"*What did you just say to me?*" the girl hisses.

"I said, *give out your own invitations,*" I repeat, before turning away from her to look at Beth. "Seriously though, can I borrow your phone to order a delivery? The smell in here is making me feel ill."

Beth is so shocked, she can't seem to find the words to reply. The girl who accosted me, however, is desperate to continue the conversation.

"Excuse me!" she says shrilly. "Aren't you going to apologize?"

"Why would I apologize to you?"

Her cheeks flush furiously. "Because you took my

party invitation and didn't deliver it to John like you said you would! Did you hide it from him just because you're not invited? That is SO immature."

"**HA!** Why would I care about being invited to *your* party?"

She narrows her eyes at me. "You shouldn't say you're going to pass on invitations, if you're going to be so petty about it."

"OK, clearly you're not going to drop this, so let's sort it now," I say in a bored voice, before clearing my throat and yelling out, "**JOHN?**"

A boy I recognize from Ruby's house earlier waves at me from across the now completely silent room. He looks VERY uncomfortable at the attention.

"Great. John, you're invited to..." I pause, turning back to the girl. "What's your name?"

Beth sniggers and the girl says, "*Ali!*" as though I've committed a terrible crime.

"John," I begin again, "you're invited to Alice's party."

"ALI!" she cries.

"Whatever. Ali's party. Did you hear that, John?"

He nods.

"There, see?" I say to Ali with a smile. "All sorted. Bye, then."

For a split second, she looks as though she's going to

either shout at me or burst into tears. Obviously deciding that neither are acceptable, she turns on her heel and marches out of the canteen with her friend behind her going, "Ali! Ali! Wait up! Are you OK?"

"Ruby, I don't know what's happened to you," Beth says, grinning as she watches Ali flounce out the room, "but whatever it is, it's BRILLIANT."

CHAPTER SEVENTEEN

(AS NAOMI)

"So," Riley begins, as we stroll through the doors of an empty shopping centre, "where would you like to start?"

This is mad. Completely and utterly **MAD**. They have closed the entire of the huge Westfield in Shepherd's Bush just so I can go shopping without being disturbed. There is no one else here except for the shop assistants, who are all standing in the doorways of the different stores waiting to see if I'll choose their one.

Oh yeah, and I can pick anything I want. For free.

Please can I never wake up from this dream?

"I guess, a clothes shop?" I say excitedly, feeling like I might pass out from all this happiness.

"What a surprise." She laughs, typing out an email on her phone. "Come on then, lead the way."

With Sam and a bodyguard a few steps behind us, we head into a designer clothes shop where the store manager greets me and then gestures to the staff standing in a straight line next to her.

"These will be your personal shoppers, Miss Starr. If you need anything at all, please just ask. They'll be happy to assist."

"Wow. Thanks!" I inhale deeply, taking in all the beautiful, posh clothes hanging neatly on rails around the brightly lit shop.

"I need to make a call about the Berlin concert tomorrow," Riley says, causing a wave of fear to wash over me. She notices my reaction. "But *you* don't need to worry about that today. Go on, go have some fun."

I don't waste any time. I wander through the empty shop like I'm in a daydream, selecting clothes I like the look of and handing them to one of the shop assistants, Andrew, who insists on carrying them for me. When his arms get too full, another assistant comes hurrying over to take those from him and carry them to the dressing room, while I continue selecting more items.

When we eventually make it to the dressing room, Andrew, with a knowing smile, puts on a Naomi Starr album, so I feel EXACTLY like I'm in one of those film montages where the main character tries on different clothes and happily dances about in them.

In real life, trying on clothes in shops is actually very tiring and boring and hot, and usually I get stuck in a jumper, with my head in one of the armholes, and Beth has to come in and help me out.

Not today, though. Today I'm a glamorous pop star and trying on clothes is a breeze.

"What do you think?" I ask Andrew, when I emerge wearing item number one of about thirty pieces waiting for me to try.

"Beautiful!" he declares, the other shop assistants nodding in agreement.

"Then I'll take it." I grin, admiring the dress in the mirror. It is the most beautiful dress I think I've ever seen: a silver-grey lace maxi dress embellished with delicate beaded flowers. As Ruby, I'd never get the opportunity to wear a dress like this, let alone be able to afford it.

But when you're Naomi Starr, you can wear whatever you like.

After a few minutes, Andrew has loaded several bags with the clothes I've decided to take and I get stuck on whether I like a pair of bright pink trousers or not.

"Can you get Riley for me? She's in the shop

somewhere," I say, examining my reflection. "I could use some advice."

He disappears and then returns to inform me that she's gone to do some work in one of the cafés with Sam.

"Do you want me to go find her?" Andrew offers.

"Oh. No, don't disturb her, it's fine."

I pull the curtain back and get changed out of them. I would ask Andrew and the other shop assistants their opinion, but so far they've answered "beautiful" to every item I've tried on, even the ones that looked really bad. I guess no one wants to risk insulting a famous pop star, but if you only ever get showered in compliments, soon enough they don't really mean much.

I wish Beth was here to give me a real opinion. I hold up the trousers and try to imagine what she'd say.

"*Duh. They're bright pink*," her voice says in my head. "*OBVIOUSLY get them!*"

I grin and stroll out, letting Andrew know I'll be taking the trousers, too.

"I'll prepare the bags for your assistants to collect. Enjoy the rest of your shopping experience, Miss Starr," he says, bowing his head slightly as I thank him and leave the shop, ready for the next one.

The bodyguard who has been accompanying me all day confirms that Riley and Sam have set up in the

Starbucks and will be there for at least the next hour or so working.

"Ms Starr asked me to pass on the message that she hopes you have a wonderful time and to head there once you're done," he explains.

"OK." My voice echoes around the deserted shopping centre. "How about handbags and shoes next?"

I realize I'm talking to myself as my bodyguard repositions himself just behind me and doesn't reply, because of course, he's doing his job, he's not here to shop. I wander into an accessories shop and can't help but smile as the waft of posh leather hits me walking through the doors. There are dozens of beautiful handbags and shoes dotted round the shop.

"Let me know if you need any assistance, Miss Starr. I'll let you shop in peace," a smartly dressed woman tells me warmly, before retreating behind the counter.

As unbelievably amazing as this experience is, it would be so much better with Beth. I feel a bit awkward, wandering around the bags and shoes on my own, knowing that everyone is watching me. I always thought that the hustle and bustle of other shoppers was irritating, but without them, it's eerily quiet and empty. I wish Riley or Sam had stuck around.

I gasp as I notice a pair of sparkly silver shoes.

"Can I try on these please?" I ask, taking one carefully from the stand. "My size is—"

"That's all right, Miss Starr," the woman behind the counter says, coming over with a fresh pair already. "I took the liberty of finding out your shoe size before you arrived today, and prepared every pair of shoes in the shop for you, ready to try on."

"Whoa," I say, taking them from her, "that is really nice of you. Thanks."

She smiles modestly and then scurries back behind the counter. I sit down and slip on the shoes, admiring them in the mirror.

"These are amazing!" I beam, looking up and then realizing that, again, I'm talking to no one.

With no one to discuss how gorgeous the shoes are, I'm not really sure what else to do but sit down and take them straight off again. The lady comes rushing over and takes the shoes away to be boxed and prepared for someone to collect when I'm done.

As I put my shoes back on in the silence, I realize that most of the fun of shopping isn't the shopping at all – it's the people you're shopping with. When Beth and I head out together, we spend most of our time cracking up with laughter as we try on stupid things, or we're super excited to buy something we've saved up for ages to get.

I have to admit that shopping on my own, even like this, where I can pick ANYTHING in the whole place, just isn't as fun.

"Right," I say, standing up and walking over to my bodyguard, who's waiting by the door, looking moody in his sunglasses. "Where next?"

Ruby, can I ask you a question?

> Oh my god, hi, Naomi! AHHH
> Naomi Starr is texting me!
> Sorry, it's still so crazy!!

By any chance, did you fall down the steps coming off my private jet as you landed in Berlin?

> No

Are you sure about that?

> Yes

Your friend Beth just showed me all these pictures on social media of ME

lying face down on the tarmac like a
STARFISH

Ah. Oh yeah! I may have had a
TINY little trip. But don't worry, no
one saw. I was so stealth about it

IT IS ALL OVER SOCIAL MEDIA.
EVERYONE SAW. THE WHOLE
WORLD SAW.

I think the thing to take away from
this is that you need to invest in some
shoes that you can actually walk in

I can walk in my shoes!! It's YOU
who can't! Now can you PLEASE
stop making me look stupid?! I have
a reputation to uphold you know.
Anyway, how are things going?
Is everything OK?

Not exactly.
Right now, I'm hiding in a cupboard

Why are you in a cupboard?

I'm hiding from your mum and the
tour manager. Also that Martin
guy, your choreographer. Who
really doesn't like you by the way.
And he DEFINITELY doesn't
like you now

Explain.

To get out of rehearsals on the arena
stage earlier during soundcheck, I told
him I was allergic to his scent

YOU WHAT?!

I panicked!!! I also tried to get
out of the concert tonight by
telling everyone I was allergic to
spotlights, but no one believed me

NO KIDDING

Have you got any ideas?? I'm running

out of time! I'm meant to be on the
stage in half an hour!

OK. Don't panic. Just say you're ill.
Really ill.

I tried that! But it turns out you have
your own private doctor who came
with us on the jet and examined me.
According to him, I'm all good.
WHAT AM I GOING TO DO?!

Ruby. You may have to go on

What? NO

It's OK. You can just say you don't
want to sing live! Then you can mime
it. You know my songs right? You said
you were a fan! Problem solved!

Yeah, but singing along to your
songs in my bedroom at home is
a bit different to singing in front of
SEVENTEEN THOUSAND PEOPLE

You can do this, Ruby. You have to
do this! For me! PLEASE. I can't miss
another concert. My career will be
OVER. Just mime, it's easy!!

I can't!!! I'm not a pop star!!
I'm a nobody!!

YOU HAVE TO DO THIS

No. No way. I can't.
I'm going to be sick

I've got to go. Your mum keeps yelling
that it's dinner time. Seriously why
do you have to all eat together at the
same time as "a family"? Ew, it is SO
cringe. Anyway, look, just do this for
me, please, Ruby? I promise you,
you're going to be great.

YOU CAN'T LEAVE ME!!
We still need to think up an excuse!
I CAN'T GO ON STAGE!

Ugh, she is telling me I have to get off my phone. Can't she see I'm busy texting? Now she's saying she's going to confiscate it if I don't come for dinner. Who does your mum think she is?! There is no way that she is going to take this phone from me and stop me from

HELLO? NAOMI?

NO MUM GIVE HER THE PHONE BACK!

NAOMI? NAOMI, ARE YOU THERE?
Help.

A sudden knock on the cupboard door makes me jump out of my skin and drop the phone.

"Naomi? Are you in there?"

"No!" I call back. "Naomi isn't in here, I'm a backing dancer. Maybe she's on the other side of the building."

"That's funny, because all the backing dancers are in position and one of the crew members saw Naomi come into this dressing room and shut herself in this very cupboard."

Busted. I push open the cupboard door and look up at Riley Starr and Sam.

"Is this some new concert preparation thing?" Riley asks, raising her eyebrows.

"Yep. That's right. Apparently, it's good luck in Europe to shut yourself in a cupboard backstage before a big show. Gather your thoughts and stuff."

"Time to get out of the cupboard, Naomi," Riley says, offering me her hand. "Your fans are waiting."

I reluctantly let her pull me to my feet.

"All right," she sighs. "Tell me what's really going on."

"You wouldn't believe me," I croak, the back of my neck sweating profusely. I can hear the muffled sound of a huge audience waiting in the arena.

"Give it a try."

She gestures for me to sit down and pulls up a chair opposite, while Sam dashes over to the fridge in the corner and gets out some bottles of water. They then both wait in patient silence for me to explain why I've been hiding in a cupboard when I should be getting ready to stroll out on to a stage and perform to thousands of fans, just like I've done pretty much my whole life with no trouble whatsoever.

I wish I could tell them. I wish I could blurt out the truth. But as Naomi and I discussed at the Ritz, no one will believe us. They'll think Naomi Starr has gone crazy.

"Naomi, whatever it is, you can tell me," Riley says, leaning forward to look into my eyes intently. "Why are you acting so strangely?"

"Um ... OK ... well, I'm..." I pause, my brain searching desperately for something to say. "I'm nervous."

"You're nervous," Riley repeats slowly. "That's what you haven't been telling me."

"Yeah. I know that sounds strange because I'm Naomi Starr. And I perform concerts all the time. But there you go. I'm nervous. Really nervous. So, I don't think I should go on."

That's when Riley acts in the strangest way. She *laughs*.

Not like a belly laugh or anything, but like a that's-no-big-deal kind of laugh.

"Naomi," she says, chuckling, "of course you're nervous! I can't believe you were worried to talk about that! We talk about it all the time!"

I stare at her, baffled. "We ... we do?"

"Oh come on, don't you remember what happened the time you played in Dublin?"

"Uh ... remind me."

"You were so nervous that you refused to go on for about an hour! The tour manager had to give you a major pep talk. And then, what about when you did your first show in New York?"

"What about it?"

"You had such bad stage fright that you forgot all the lyrics to your first two songs. You just danced instead and then ran off and burst into tears! Oh, and the time you performed at the MTV awards—"

"Wait, I remember that! I was amazing then! That was one of my best performances!" I hesitate, realizing how that sounds. "I mean, that's what people told me."

"You were amazing. Absolutely brilliant," Riley assures me, Sam nodding in the background. "But don't you remember what you were saying to me before? You kept saying over and over, 'Mum, I can't do this. I can't do this.' It took a lot of persuading to get you on that stage."

I can't believe what I'm hearing. Naomi Starr gets *nervous*? But she always looks so confident on stage. How is this possible?

"The nerves give you adrenaline," Riley continues, as though reading my mind. "The best and most famous stars in history often get nervous. It's natural! But sometimes you have to face your fears to do what you love and show who you are."

"OK, but what if tonight it's different? What if tonight, it's not just nerves?" I take a deep breath. "What if I don't feel like Naomi Starr? I don't feel like a pop star. I feel like a nobody. A nobody who doesn't have the talent or confidence to sing in front of her family, let alone thousands of people."

She reaches over and takes my hand. "Well, then I would say that maybe you need to have a little more faith in yourself. Wouldn't you agree, Sam?"

"Absolutely," he says cheerily. "You may not feel like a pop star, but you sure look like one to me."

I smile gratefully at him and Riley squeezes my hand.

"You can do this," she says, and then before I can protest, she drags me to my feet and suddenly we're marching out of the dressing room and down the maze of backstage corridors towards the wings leading out on to the stage.

The crowd is chanting Naomi's name in excitement. I feel completely numb with fear. Someone is fitting my earpiece while someone else places a glittery microphone into my hand.

I don't know what to do. I glance over my shoulder and see a crowd of backstage crew and dancers standing behind me, blocking my exit. There's no chance of me making a run for it.

I quickly turn to Riley, who is standing next to me and speaking into a headset.

"Wait. I can't do this," I tell her, my hands shaking. "This is all wrong. I'm not Naomi."

"Do you remember when you used to dance around your bedroom, pretending you were a pop star?" she says in response, ignoring me completely.

"Huh?"

"Do you?"

"Um. Well, yeah."

If only she knew I was doing that just a few days ago.

"Forget the crowd out there," she tells me. "That stage is your bedroom. Go sing and dance just like you love to do. Show everyone how you shine."

I blink at her. *W-what did you just say?*

"You are a pop star. Everyone else can see that. You just have to believe it," she beams. "Let that pop star inside of you shine!"

The lights go down. The audience erupts. Riley wishes me good luck and gently guides me out of the wings. The band starts up and a spotlight shines down, an empty pool of light waiting centre-stage.

Treading in Naomi Starr's shoes, I walk out towards it.

I turn to face the audience, a sea of faces that goes so

far back, I can't see the end of the crowd. They go crazy as I get into the spotlight and squint out at them. The noise is so deafening that I stumble backwards. There are thousands of blinking phone lights all shining up at me expectantly.

I'm frozen. Completely frozen. My heart is slamming hard against my chest. My throat is closing up in fear.

And I realize now that I forgot to say that I wouldn't sing live.

The band is playing the introduction to one of Naomi's songs. It's 'Shining Bright'. One of my favourites. As I stand frozen to the spot and the band repeats the introduction, waiting for me to come in, I hear a voice yell to me from the wings. It's Riley.

"You can do this!" she's shouting, beaming at me as though I'm not messing up a huge arena concert right now. "You're Naomi Starr!"

That's when a thought flits through my mind:

Maybe, just maybe, I can do this.

Because Riley is right. I'm not Ruby, the clumsy, shy nobody right now. The crowd can't see Ruby up on this stage. They can see *Naomi Starr*. I just have to pretend to be her.

I lift the microphone to my lips and I start to sing.

There's an eruption of cheers as soon as I start

singing, and it gives me a boost of confidence. This might actually be working. As the song goes on, I start relaxing into it a bit more. I notice the dancers around me doing a routine and I recognize it from the music video of this song. I know all the steps.

I can do this.

As we hit the chorus, I find the courage to go for it. I launch into the dance routine, pretending I'm in my bedroom dancing around to Naomi's song, my only audience member Daisy, lounging on my bed, chewing happily on one of Roman's shoes that he's left lying around.

It works. I dance perfectly in time with my dancers, while singing all the lyrics. And when the song ends and we strike our final pose, the crowd's reaction is so overwhelming, it feels like the whole world is cheering for me. Confetti cannons go off from the ceiling and glitter rains down around me as I attempt to catch my breath, tears rolling down my cheeks. This must be the best, most incredible feeling in the world.

I can't believe it. I can't believe what just happened.

I did it.

CHAPTER EIGHTEEN

NAOMI

(AS RUBY)

"If you don't give my phone back, I am going to **SUE**. Did you hear me? I mean it! **I WILL SUE YOU AND YOUR ENTIRE FAMILY!**"

I'm yelling at the top of my lungs, but it's like I'm invisible. I even try waving my arms around while shouting to see if that gets anyone's attention, but no one notices and then one of the gross boys of this dysfunctional family shoves me out of the way as he steals the seat I was about to sit at.

This is the WORST.

I can't believe I am stuck here in this house of

crazy. I should be in Berlin right now performing to my thousands of adoring fans.

"Stop talking about suing people and sit down, Ruby," John says, putting his book aside for a moment to spoon peas on to his plate. "You're being weird."

"How dare you! I am **NOT** weird. I am an icon, John! An icon!"

So far, John is the only one of Ruby's hundreds of siblings that I can remember the name of and that's because of the canteen showdown with Ali yesterday at school. He seems to spend most of his time reading, so I don't know how he can possibly think that *I* am the weird one around here.

I am so over this whole body swap thing.

Not only have I had to sleep in Ruby's tiny bedroom and put up with her strange family and her stinky dog, I have had to suffer two days of school. TWO DAYS. I don't think I'll be able to survive another one.

For one thing, the teachers won't stop yelling at me, even for the tiniest things. I brought the wrong textbooks to class and it was this **HUGE** deal, and I got in trouble for speaking without putting my hand up first. If that wasn't bad enough, I discovered that you have to *ask the teacher's permission* to go to the toilet during their lesson. It's the stupidest thing I've ever heard! I swear, if

I wasn't so busy writing and recording platinum-selling and award-winning albums, I'd be writing to the prime minister or whoever and telling them that they have GOT to sort out this whole asking-to-go-to-the-toilet thing in schools.

Plus, the lessons go on FOR EVER. Who has that kind of attention span? I keep getting told off for looking out of the window or yawning (I admit, I did yawn loudly a couple of times on purpose because I thought it was constructive criticism).

And don't get me started on the food served in the canteen. It should be illegal. There's no way round it either. I tried ordering in some sashimi and the school receptionist sent away the delivery driver, so I had no choice but to starve.

Also, you have ZERO freedom. Yesterday, the bell FINALLY rang for the end of school and I was like, "See ya," to Beth, and she went, "Wait, don't you have detention from Mr Jones?"

"Oh yeah. What does that mean exactly?" I asked.

"It means you have to go to his classroom and sit there for another hour working in silence."

YEAH RIGHT! I laughed right in her face at that one and then left the school pronto. The fact that I'd stayed until the end of school was a miracle; I wasn't going to extend the torture. And then do you know what happened? I walked into school this morning and Mr Jones, aka the Angry Ferret, comes storming over and tells me that for missing detention, I get **ANOTHER DETENTION**.

I told him no, thanks. I was already in a bad mood because I had woken up still in Ruby's body and been forced to get on a smelly overcrowded bus and go to school yet again.

Then he said, "Well then, you'll be getting another detention!"

"And if I don't show up to any of the detentions, what then?" I told him. "Will you just give me more detentions that I won't attend? Looks like your punishment system is severely flawed. Anyway, I have to go wash my hands now because I've just been on the bus and it was disgusting. NO ONE respects your personal space on that thing. I plan on suing the bus company because I'm almost certain that whoever stepped on my foot as they got off broke all of my toes."

Apparently, speaking back to Mr Jones and then ranting about the bus was "unacceptable behaviour" and I got sent to the headmaster's office where he lectured me for about half an hour, but I wasn't listening because I was distracted by his strange obsession with owls.

Literally everything in his office had an owl on it. There was an owl clock, an owl paperweight and an owl painting on the wall. Even the pen he was signing papers with had a fluffy owl on the end. Weirdo.

Anyway, this whole school experience has made me super appreciative of my personal tutor, Harry, who comes with me on world tours and gives me lessons whenever I have free time, because it's the law or whatever.

He never makes me do homework and I can get away with pretty much everything, even texting or scrolling through Instagram while he's teaching.

I think he may be a little bit frightened of me because of the time I knocked everything off the desk in protest at being asked a question about the periodic table when I was trying to write a song verse.

I had the best lyric in my head and then his stupid repeated question about the symbol for iron made me forget it.

"Ruby, please sit down," Ruby's mum, Callie, says, barely looking up from the manuscript on her lap. "Everyone dig in."

"How was everyone's day?" Ruby's dad asks, but everyone is too busy eating or talking over him to answer.

I reluctantly sit down at the end of the table, glaring at Callie, still annoyed at her for taking the phone away. As soon as I take my seat, that scruffy dog comes bounding over with her gross tongue lolling out, trying to get me to pet her.

"Back to your bed!" I instruct, keeping my hands up away from her before she can slobber over me. "Off you go! Back to your bed! Leave me alone! Ugh! WHY doesn't she understand what I'm saying?"

"Because she's a dog, you loser," one of the identical twins says, piling an abnormal amount of potatoes on to his plate.

I wrinkle my nose at the food on the table. No offence to Ruby's parents, I'm sure it's great, but this is not Michelin-star-chef standard like I'm used to.

"Excuse me, Callie and/or Anthony?" I say, addressing Ruby's parents. "Do you have any green juice in the house at all? I really need it for my skin. It's suffering because of school in general."

But they don't hear me. In fact, I can barely hear myself over the noise at this table. The twins have already got in an argument about a sports lesson they had at school today; the eldest son is debating with his dad about some DNA-related news bulletin today; and John has asked his mum's opinion on the current number-one non-fiction book.

This is EXACTLY what happened at yesterday's dinner.

"**HELLO!**" I huff, slamming my cutlery on the table. "Can someone **PLEASE** listen to me?"

"You know what, Reggie, when that ball hit your head in football today, it must have knocked out your brain cells," a twin is saying. "The score was two-one to MY team."

"It was four-three to MY team, Roman," Reggie replies. "You can't make up scores!"

"Yes, but Dad, medical research has proven that not to be necessarily true," the eldest boy is saying across the twins, with his mouth full, I might add. "Didn't you read the news today?"

"I did, and I think that the recent findings are problematic," Anthony replies, passing the bowl of salad to his wife on autopilot.

She has no idea he's holding it out for her and is deep in conversation with John.

Anthony doesn't seem to notice she hasn't taken it from him and so just continues to hold the salad bowl up for the entirety of the meal.

"I don't understand why you're brushing aside twenty-first century fiction!" Callie is saying to John, a fork in one hand, a pen in the other. "You seem to be boldly prioritizing other periods with very little thought process!"

"I'm not prioritizing Shakespeare, Mum," John replies

with a sigh. "It's the school syllabus. I have to learn what I'm told to learn."

"Ah, now *that's* an interesting debate."

"EXCUSE ME!" I yell, before being nudged on the arm by a cold wet nose. "EW, DAISY! Go away! Back to your bed!"

She ignores my instructions and instead rests her head on my lap, looking up at me with those stupid big eyes.

"Fine, you can stay there," I grumble. "But don't get used to it, you gross slobberer."

"MY TEAM WON!" Roman yells, slamming his fork on the table. "Mum, tell him my team won!"

"Yes, sweetheart, help yourself to peas," she replies, brushing him off before turning her attention back to John. "You need to start standing your ground and thinking for yourself. Do you want to be a puppet, told what books to study and how to think?"

"Mum wasn't there, Roman!" Reggie cries. "But I was there and I can tell you that his team LOST!"

"Can someone PLEASE tell me where I can get some healthy juice around here?" I ask again, waving my arms.

"Reggie, do you need to spit when you yell?" the eldest boy says, wiping his cheek in disgust.

"I will spit when I yell passionately, Jeroame!" Reggie

responds. "And I'm yelling passionately because Roman is a liar!"

"Keep your voices down, please. Let's stay calm," their dad says, chuckling. "I'm all for competitive nature but let's remember good sportsmanship."

"It's not me being the sore loser, Dad! It's Reggie!" Roman says.

"I heard that Roman's team won, if that helps," John chips in.

"SHUT UP, JOHN!" Reggie shouts, while Roman yells, "**AHA!**" at the same time.

"Green juice! Anyone!" I attempt again.

"I heard that Reggie's team won," Jeroame offers.

"SHUT UP, JEROAME!" Roman yells, while Reggie does a little dance with his arms. "Stop dancing like that, Reggie, you look stupid!"

"You look stupid!"

Roman picks up a boiled potato from his plate and throws it at Reggie, but it misses and hits John on the head. John retaliates by throwing a carrot at Roman, but misses and instead hits Jeroame. Jeroame then scoops a spoonful of peas up and throws them at John, but misses and hits Reggie. Reggie picks up a handful of cabbage and throws it at Jeroame, but misses and. . .

SPLAT!

"**AHHHHHHHHH!**" I jump to my feet as wet cabbage hits me in the face.

The dog thinks that I'm getting up to play and starts barking excitedly, jumping up and down at me.

"All right, enough of the food throwing!" Ruby's mum demands. "Someone hand Ruby a napkin. Now!"

But I don't need a napkin. Oh no. **I NEED REVENGE!**

Without a moment's hesitation, I grab some boiled potatoes from the bowl in the middle and throw them at Reggie. All three of them hit him right in the face.

"THERE! How do you like it, huh?" I yell, seething as I pick cabbage out of my hair. "NOW you can pass me a napkin!"

For a moment, everyone at the table stares at me in stunned silence. Then, they all burst out laughing. Even Ruby's parents look impressed. John passes me a napkin, chuckling, while Jeroame gives me a thumbs up.

"Nice shot, Ruby!" Roman says, while Reggie applauds me, a bit of potato still on his forehead. "Who knew you had it in you?"

They all grin at me as I calmly sit back down and everyone resumes eating.

And even though I have cabbage in my hair and dog slobber all over my skirt, and it looks like no one is bringing me a fresh green juice any time soon, I find myself grinning back at this outrageous, noisy, mad family.

I can't help it.

CHAPTER NINETEEN

RUBY

(AS NAOMI)

**You were BRILLIANT!!
Thank you so much!!
YOU DID IT!! I had a
feeling you could xx**

I feel like my heart might burst when I read Naomi's message. I put the phone down on the table and exhale, enjoying the moment's silence of being in my dressing room alone, taking in everything that just happened.

I've never felt like this before. Like I can't stop smiling. My ears are still ringing from the noise of the crowd when the concert ended and the adrenaline rush from all the dancing hasn't finished. I've never performed in front of **ANYONE** before in my whole life and I've just stepped off stage from singing and dancing in an **ARENA** concert to **THOUSANDS** of people.

And the best part is: it wasn't me.

And that's why I could get over my fear and do the show. Because it wasn't Ruby, the nobody, up on the stage; it was Naomi Starr, the biggest pop star on the planet! Nobody was going to laugh at her or ask what she was doing centre stage.

I look longingly at the phone on the table and WISH I could phone my family. I wish I could tell Mum and Dad about the show. I wish I could tell my brothers and Isabella. And I really WISH I could tell Beth. I've never wanted to jump up and down and scream in happiness more, and yet I have no one to jump up and down and scream with me.

When I stepped off stage, Riley gave me the biggest hug ever and told me how proud she was and how brilliant I'd been, but then she had to rush off to manage some admin about whatever we have to do next. And I found myself just standing there backstage, looking around for someone to celebrate with. Anyone.

But the backing dancers were all hugging and high-fiving each other. None of them approached me. Sam was busy fetching me some sparkling elderflower that apparently I always have when I come off stage.

"Great show, Naomi," the sound engineer said, as he came to take away my microphone and earpiece. "You're a real star."

"Oh, thanks so much, it's such an amazing feeling, I don't think I've ever. . ."

"Yes, Mike, I'm getting it now and then I'll be right there."

My sentence trailed off as he started talking to someone through his headset. So I came here to my dressing room to sit by myself, surrounded by the vases bursting with flowers, sent from fans and famous friends.

There's a knock on the door and Sam comes in carrying my sparkling elderflower, accompanied by Naomi's stylist.

"Are you ready to get dressed for the after-party?" he asks as the stylist starts riffling through a rail of beautiful dresses.

"I get to go to an after-party?" I squeal, forgetting that it wouldn't be a big deal for the real Naomi.

"It's being thrown in your honour at your hotel – the most luxurious hotel in Berlin, of course." He checks something on his iPad. "You have ten minutes until the car will be here to take you. Do you need anything else at all? Can I get you another drink?"

"No thanks, Sam. I'm just glad that we're having a party, it will be nice to thank all my dancers and speak to everyone who put the show together," I enthuse.

There's another knock on the door and several more women come in: my hair stylist and a couple of people who seem to be here just to help me get undressed and then dressed again. As we continue talking, one of them starts unlacing my boots for me. It's kind of weird.

"Oh, they won't be coming to your party," Sam says, still looking at his iPad. "They have their own one as usual."

"Wait, what do you mean?" I ask, trying to keep my balance as the woman at my feet attempts to remove one of the boots without any luck. "Um, thanks so much, but I can take off my own shoes."

She ignores me and continues to loosen the laces, while I wobble around unsteadily.

"The crew and dancers have their own after-party organized by the tour manager," Sam explains. "Theirs is a bit more . . . casual."

"But why wouldn't I go to that after-party? Surely the point is to celebrate the big show we've just put on together. Aren't they invited to this party I'm going to?"

Sam blinks at me, starting to look nervous again. I've noticed in the past couple of days that he's grown in confidence a bit. When I mentioned it to Riley, she said simply, "I think that's because you're calling him by his actual name."

"No, they're not invited," he says. "But I think they would rather do their own thing anyway."

"Oh. OK. So, if they're not coming, then who will I know at this party?"

"There are some very big names on the list." He holds out the tablet so I can see the names on the screen. "Only A-listers invited and almost all of them said yes."

"This is going to sound strange, but do I actually *know* anyone on this list? As in, is anyone there who is my friend?"

He studies the screen before eventually saying, "Not really, but I think you met this prince once? Oh no, wait, I think that was a different prince."

"I'm sorry, Miss Starr, we now only have eight minutes until your car arrives," the stylist points out, holding up two dresses. "Which one do you think?"

But before I can choose, my left boot is yanked off without warning and I go toppling backwards into the dressing table, sending flowers flying everywhere.

The door of the sleek black car is opened and I step out on to the red carpet. There are photographers jostling to get to the front of the rope cordoning off the carpet and as soon as my head emerges from the car, the flashes start going off.

I'm a little more prepared for it this time and even manage a cheery little wave. I realize once I get into the hotel that most stars don't wave at photographers but do sophisticated, pouty poses.

I'll have to work on that.

"Oh my goodness, Naomi, you were the BEST tonight!" a woman says as soon as I step into the party, giving me two air kisses. I think I recognize her from TV. "I was in Germany filming for my new drama and I just HAD to get tickets when I heard you were performing here! I am such a fan. Are you wearing Marina Blair? She is literally my favourite designer. I can't believe you ruined her fashion show like you did. So outrageous, I love it. Oh, there's Adam, I must go say hi. I'll find you later!"

"Uh, OK, bye!" I say, not sure what just happened.

"Naomi, there you are," Riley says, tottering over to me in the most amazing high heels I've ever seen and looking like she's just stepped out of *Vogue* magazine. She has to be the coolest mum on the planet. "Has someone got you a drink? What would you like, sparkling elderflower?"

"I'll get one right away," Sam states, lurking nearby at all times.

He darts off before I can agree to it or not.

"There's a few people who want to meet you," Riley says, beckoning over several stylish and intimidating-looking guests. "They're big fans and important people in the industry. It will be good for you to chat to them while I go sort some last-minute scheduling problems for tomorrow. Remember, Naomi, networking is key in this business."

"What's happening tomorrow? I thought that I might be able to see some of Berlin," I say hopefully. "We could go see some sights together."

"I wish." She laughs. "But we don't have time. Tomorrow we fly back to London first thing and you have a photo shoot, then two interviews, followed by filming for a skincare advert and then you're on a chat show. And of course, now you performed so amazingly this evening, your record label is begging for a meeting. I guess they've forgiven you for skipping out on the London concert. They want to rearrange it for this weekend but we have to see if that's in any way possible."

"Whoa. That all sounds ... intense."

"I know, right? At least you don't have to worry about the admin side. That's my job." She turns to smile at the guests waiting to introduce themselves. "Now, enjoy your party. You deserve it!"

I've never been to a celebrity party before, but I've spent plenty of time lost in daydreams about attending one, usually during double maths when Mr Jones is droning on. This is just as glitzy and glamorous as I imagined. Everyone in the room is someone important and they're all wearing beautiful clothes and sparkly jewellery. They're all laughing and chatting and having their pictures taken by the official photographer, while cool music plays in the background and waiters weave through the crowd with trays of tiny, posh canapés. It's absolutely **AMAZING**. Just how I always dreamed it.

The thing is, I imagined it would be more fun.

I don't want to sound ungrateful because this is the most incredible event I've ever been to and there's no way I'll ever go to anything like this again. It's just, I've spoken to everyone I've been told to speak to and smiled for a hundred photos, but I'm not really around anyone long enough to have a proper chat. It's like musical chairs, but with party guests. They seem to be talking at me rather than with me before disappearing to talk at someone else.

"Sam?" I say after a while, when my feet are really aching. "Is it time to go home yet?"

"Actually, according to your schedule, you will be leaving the party in five minutes."

"Oh. Well, I'm ready now, if that's OK."

He holds out a room key. "Of course, here's the key to your suite. And you'll be receiving your wake-up call at three a.m."

"What?" My jaw drops open. "That early?"

"Your car will be here at three-thirty a.m. to take you to the private jet so we can get back to London on time, before a busy day begins. Your team of stylists will be on the plane so don't worry, you'll be ready by the time we land."

"But . . . I'm so tired after the concert. . ."

I trail off, not sure what I'm expecting. I check myself. This is Naomi's pop star life and I have no right to meddle.

"Sorry. Yes, three a.m. wake-up call sounds great."

I thank him for the room key and then slide out of the room, without anyone noticing that I've left. Which is strange considering it's a party in my honour.

The concierge notices me heading towards the stairs and insists on having someone show me to my room even though I point out it's only one floor up and I don't have any luggage to carry. But still, I'm accompanied by several porters, who all walk along with me in professional silence and even take the key from me to unlock the door, just in case my hand is too tired to lift it to the lock or whatever.

"Wow!" I gasp when I walk into my suite.

It's **HUGE**. Basically the size of our house. And it's so beautiful. Sparkling chandeliers, vases of white roses dotted around on the polished tables and the biggest bed I've ever seen. My suitcase is already here waiting for me, not that I know what's in it. Before we got in the car to get to the private jet, I mentioned to Riley that I needed to pack and she laughed, thinking I was telling a hilarious joke.

It turns out that Naomi Starr never packs her own case.

I thank the porters and then, after I've shut the door, I take a good run-up and hurtle towards the bed, landing sprawled out on all the silk cushions. I giggle into the sheets and then roll over to lie on my back, staring up at the ceiling.

I suddenly get an overwhelming feeling of missing Beth.

She would **LOVE** this place. We would be screaming, running around it and then jumping up and down on the bed. We'd be ordering a load of room service and then settling in to watch movies all night on the TV, which is the size of a small cinema screen, snug in our personalized dressing gowns.

Once I was round Beth's house for a sleepover and she went into the bathroom to shower and came out wearing a fluffy white dressing gown with matching fluffy white slippers and a fluffy white towel in a turban on her head.

"Do you like my outfit?" she'd asked, striking a pose. "Dad stole this stuff from a posh hotel. It's so nice, I reckon I could get away with wearing it out and about."

"Yeah, sure," I'd said, laughing.

She'd raised her eyebrows in that challenge-accepted way she does. "Oh, you don't think I'd wear this outside?"

"No, obviously not. It's a dressing gown."

She'd then given me a sly smile before turning on her heel and marching out of the room and down the stairs, and the next thing I knew, she was heading out of the front door. She ended up walking all the way down the road to the bus stop, waving happily at neighbours she passed along the way. The best moment was when our head teacher drove past in his car and slammed on his brakes when he saw her.

"Good evening to you, headmaster!" she'd said

brightly, strolling along the pavement as he looked at her in horror.

I'd laughed so hard, I'd almost peed myself.

I check Naomi's phone to see if anyone has messaged to congratulate me for the concert but there's no new texts. I wonder if anyone has ever made Naomi laugh so hard that she's almost peed herself. Judging by what I've seen of her world so far, it seems pretty unlikely.

She's missing out.

Too tired to move, I close my eyes for a minute. This bedroom really is the most beautiful room in the world, but I can't help thinking that a scruffy dog on the bed, chewing someone's shoe and taking up most of the space, would make it just that much better.

CHAPTER TWENTY

NAOMI

(AS RUBY)

Beth scrunches up her face and puts on a voice.

"If you answer me back one more time, Ruby, I'm going to give you detention! Again!"

I laugh so hard that the coconut water I'm drinking goes right up my nose.

"AHH!" I yelp, pinching my nose and grabbing a napkin from her lunch tray while Beth giggles. "You made it go up my nose! It feels so weird!"

"I told you my Mr Jones impression was uncanny," she says proudly. "And you doubted me."

"That was amazing," I admit, wiping tears from my

eyes. "I don't think I've ever laughed so hard into a drink before that it actually went up my nose."

"What are you talking about? Don't you remember when you were drinking that cup of tea at my house and I walked into the door?" She chuckles at the memory. "You made me look like the elegant one when you started jumping about going, 'Hot water up my nose! Hot water up my nose!'"

I smile, picking up my fork and stabbing at my salad. "You know, the food isn't too bad today."

"OK, that's it," Beth says, leaning forward on the table. "What's going on?"

"What do you mean?"

"It's the first time all week you haven't complained about your tray being wet. When I passed it to you, you didn't say one word. You just took it."

"Huh." I look down at the damp tray. "Yeah, I didn't really notice."

"And now you're saying the food's not too bad today." Beth narrows her eyes at me. "Is the diva side of you that you've been bringing out this week suddenly disappearing again? If so, then please can you annoy Mr Jones one more time before you go back to saying nothing in class? I need to study his angry features a little more before my impression is absolutely spot on."

I consider Beth's point. Maybe I'm letting things slide today because I'm getting a little more used to waking up in a mad house with Daisy slobbering in my face.

Or maybe it's because I FINALLY had a hot shower this morning.

I came up with a genius solution, and if I hadn't won Best Music Video at the VMAs earlier this year, it probably would have been my proudest achievement to date. Yesterday when I eventually got my turn in the shower and the boys had used up the hot water AGAIN, I vowed to myself that this would not happen any more.

There was no point in trying to talk to them about it. Action needed to be taken.

So last night, I found the toolbox under the sink in the kitchen and set to work. This morning when everyone's alarms went off and Roman rushed to beat Reggie to the shower, he discovered no lock on the door.

"HEY!" he shouted, waking up the whole house. **"WHO TOOK THE LOCK OFF THE BATHROOM DOOR?"**

"I did," I announced triumphantly, standing in my doorway, holding up the lock in my hand.

The rest of the family emerged from their rooms to find out what was going on and I gleefully filled them in.

"I have removed the bathroom door lock because I am tired of having COLD showers and I will not stand for it one day longer. You boys are having long showers and taking all the hot water which is very SELFISH." I pointed at each of them in turn with the lock. "So, this is what's going to happen. Showers will now be timed. Five minutes each. That is sufficient time for everyone to bathe. And when your time is up, if you are not out of the shower, then I will be coming right on in there and dragging you out. Does everyone understand?"

They all stared at me in stunned silence. Callie had started to slow clap.

"That's my girl, Ruby," she said, beaming at me. "You heard her, boys. In you go, Roman, your five minutes start now."

He scurried into the bathroom, and when the alarm went off on my phone, I kicked open the door and he jumped out of that shower like a shot.

It was a magnificent start to the day.

"Did you see your favourite pop star on Instagram?" Beth says, jolting me from my smug thoughts.

"Who?"

"Naomi Starr, obviously. Haven't you seen what she's done to her hair? Turns out, I'm a trendsetter."

"What do you mean? What's she done to her hair?"

I ask, my voice getting higher and higher with the rising panic. "She hasn't touched it, right?"

Beth scrolls through her phone and then holds it up so I can see the screen. I shriek, causing everyone in the canteen to turn and stare at us.

"She's dyed it PINK?" I yell, looking at the picture. "**HOW DARE SHE!**"

"I think it looks cool," Beth says, laughing at my reaction. "It really suits her."

"She is in SO much trouble," I declare, angrily reaching for my phone and typing a text.

**WHAT HAVE YOU DONE
TO MY HAIR?!
EXPLAIN YOURSELF AT ONCE.**

"Whoa, calm down." Beth gives me a strange look and I realize I haven't hidden my true self all that well. "Does it really bother you that much?"

"No, obviously not," I say hurriedly, putting my phone down and clearing my throat. "It's not like I know her. It's not like I care what Naomi Starr does to her hair. I mean, it's her hair. So, nothing to do with me. I might dye my hair bright neon green. See how she likes it."

"Firstly, I'm not sure Naomi Starr would ever get the

chance to see your green hair, and secondly, you'd be in even more trouble than you are now," Beth points out. "I've been told that if my hair isn't back to its normal colour after this weekend, I'll be suspended. Trust me, it's not worth the hassle."

I'm about to tell her that I don't care about any of that when someone knocks into my back, almost causing me to face plant my salad. I swivel in my seat to find that Ali person smiling too widely down at me.

"Oops. So sorry, Ruby, didn't see you there," she says, before sauntering out of the canteen, giggling and whispering with that friend, Charlotte, who always follows her.

"Seriously, why does she think she runs this school?" I ask Beth, irritated.

"Ignore her," Beth advises, glaring at her back. "She's just overconfident because it's the auditions now. She's full of herself today."

"Auditions? For what?"

"Are you serious?" Beth rolls her eyes. "The talent show! What is with your memory lately?"

"Oh right, the talent show. And that's a big deal?"

"You know it is, especially to Ali. Why do you think she's having her big party next Saturday? The talent show is Friday night and so she plans on winning the trophy and then celebrating herself the next day. It's sickening."

"Why are you so sure she'll win?"

"Because she always wins. It pains me to say, but she's quite good at singing and dancing." Beth takes a sip of her water, watching me closely. She must notice my intrigued expression, because she adds, "Of course, she's not as good as you."

I know Ruby is good at singing and dancing. I've seen her on stage. Her performance in Berlin is all over YouTube and she's performed a couple of songs on chat shows since then. She's *brilliant*.

But her family haven't mentioned anything about her talents. It's like she's kept them a secret. And from the texts she sent me before the Berlin concert, I gathered that she's not mad about being on stage.

"You think I'm good at singing and dancing?" I ask casually.

"I've told you a hundred times," Beth says in hushed tones. "But you refuse to do the talent show! If people could see what you could do, there's no chance Ali would win."

"And I refuse to do the talent show because" – I have a go at guessing – "I'm too nervous? Too scared? Have stage fright?"

"I don't know why you have it in your head that people won't take you seriously. I wish you'd believe in yourself a bit more."

I take a sip of my drink, a plan brewing in my brain. I feel excited. Because if I pulled this off, I wouldn't just be having fun, I'd also be helping Ruby. And I'd be helping the whole school if I knocked Ali off her perch. I slam my glass down on the table.

"Beth, you're right. I do need to believe in myself a bit more."

"Yeah. You do."

"So, let's go."

"What? Where?"

I stand, pick up my tray and grin at her. "To the talent show auditions."

The first few rows of the auditorium are filled by the time we get there and there's a teacher standing on the stage, outlining the process. Beth and I slide into two seats at the back until she's done.

"As many of you already know, there will be six final acts who will go through to the talent show next Friday. The judging panel is myself, the headmaster and Mr Jones."

My nemesis! I grimace. This isn't a great start.

"We are going to call you up on the stage one by one, in no particular order," she continues. "Please announce your name and your talent before you begin. So, let's have a look at my list..." She checks the sign-up sheet on her clipboard. "Ali Carlton, you're up."

"You need to go now," Beth encourages as the teacher walks down the steps to take her seat in the front row. "You have to persuade her to let you audition."

"Got it."

We get up and race down the aisle to the three judges, who look startled to see us.

"Mrs Jennings, Ruby would like to audition too," Beth announces before I can, which is very handy because now I know the name of the teacher.

"Who?"

"Me. Ruby." I give her a winning smile. "I would like to audition please."

"Oh!" She slides her glasses up her nose and examines the clipboard. "I don't seem to have your name down on the sign-up list."

"No, that's because at first I was too nervous to sign up. But here I am, ready to go. I will be singing and also dancing. At the same time."

I sound like such a loser. Ruby must have started to rub off on me.

Mr Jones shifts in his seat, already irritated by my mere presence. The headmaster looks as though he doesn't really care that much, and considering he's already checking his owl watch, I'm guessing that he's hoping this is all over speedily.

Beth reaches into her bag and pulls out a camera. "And if you let Ruby go on, I can stick around to take photos of the auditions for the school paper. Great publicity, right?"

That grabs the headmaster's attention and he looks up.

"What a good idea," he tells Mrs Jennings. "We should promote our support of the arts."

"You're really supposed to sign up," Mrs Jennings says. "We have a lot of people to get through."

"Is this some kind of JOKE?" a shrill voice asks from the stage. We spin round to see Ali looming over us, her hands on her hips. "She didn't sign up, so she's not allowed to audition. Rules are rules."

"Scared of a little competition, Alice?" I ask.

Her eyes bulge out of her head. "My name is ALI! And I'm not in the least bit scared of someone like *you*."

"There you go then." I shrug. "So no one objects to me auditioning."

"I suppose it's always nice to see new faces in the

theatre," Mrs Jennings muses. "I didn't realize you were interested in singing or dancing, Ruby."

"I've kept it secret for maximum audition impact. Everyone loves an underdog, right?"

Seriously, what am I even saying?

But it seems to work, because Mrs Jennings smiles at me before writing Ruby's name down on her list.

"All right, then," she says, gesturing for us to take a seat. "You can prepare to audition."

"YES!" Beth says and holds up her hand expectantly.

It takes me a second to realize what she's doing and I stare at her hand. Then it hits me. She's waiting for me to high-five her! Feeling a rush of excitement, I eagerly comply. All my backing dancers and crew high-five each other after shows, but no one ever high-fives me.

Who knew such a small gesture would make me feel so giddy?

I need to be careful. I really am turning into a loser.

"This is NOT FAIR!" Ali whines as Beth and I take our seats. "Everyone else bothered to sign up."

"Get on with your audition, Ali," Mrs Jennings says in a tired voice, causing Ali to look mortified.

"What are you going to sing?" Beth whispers to me. "I'll download the backing music on my phone now and we can plug it into the PA system."

"Naomi Starr, 'Shining Bright'," I reply without hesitation, feeling the familiar tingle of nerves and excitement in my hands that I get before I sing.

You'd think I'd be used to performing by now but, no matter how big or small the audience, I always get hit by a wave of fear before going on stage. It's never gone away.

"A very relevant song choice," Beth says, scrolling through her phone. "Time for everyone to see how you shine."

I turn to stare at her. "W-what did you just say?"

She laughs at my expression. "I know it sounds cheesy, but I mean it. Haven't you always felt a bit like you've been on the sidelines?"

The lights dim and Ali starts her performance. I'm distracted by what Beth has said, because she's right. I know she was talking about Ruby, but somehow her words also resonate with me.

Even though I'm a pop star and I get everything I want at the drop of a hat, I've always felt like I'm missing out on something. Every time I walk off that stage and I pass a dancer or a musician high-fiving another member of the crew on the way to my dressing room, where I sit alone, I feel like I'm on the sidelines, waiting for someone to tell me what to do or say next.

I sink down in my seat, blinking back tears. I wish Mum was here.

CHAPTER TWENTY-ONE

RUBY

(AS NAOMI)

Standing alone backstage, I watch the dancers link arms in a huddle, ready for Martin to give them their pre-show pep talk. I consider wandering over and asking to join in, because I could really use some words of support and encouragement right now, but I know Naomi never does that and I have to be in character. I tear my eyes away from them.

"Naomi, have you got everything you need?" Riley appears at my side with a headset on. "You're on in about twenty minutes."

It's the live final of a new TV talent show and I'm about to perform as the music act. Earlier I peered out from the wings; the audience is huge and there are cameras everywhere. I try to steady my breathing, shaking out my hands as the nerves tingle through my fingers, reminding myself that I've done this a few times this week. I am simply playing a part. It's a dream that will soon be over, so I have to give it all I've got.

I am Naomi Starr. I'm a famous pop star. I'm doing what I love. I'm singing and—

"Did they mention to you about the competition winners?" Riley suddenly asks, noticing a crew member leading a large group of people towards us.

He waves awkwardly and Riley mouths "one minute" at him.

"Everyone who was supposed to see you at the London concert you missed was entered into a competition for tickets to the live final today," she explains, turning back to me. "They've got a meet and greet with you now quickly and then they'll go take their seats ready for your performance. Sorry, I thought someone had filled you in."

"I have to meet them now?" I bite my lip. "I'm too nervous to really talk to anyone."

"It will only be quick," she assures me. "Just say hello, thank them for coming and take some pictures."

I reluctantly follow her over. The man in charge of the

group steps aside and excitedly announces to the group, "Here she is, Naomi Starr!"

There's a lot of squealing and gasping, and they all hold up their phones. I stop suddenly, my breath catching in my throat. Riley gives me a strange look.

"Are you OK?" she whispers.

I'm not OK. I'm not at all OK. Because standing at the front of the group, jumping up and down with excitement is *Ali Carlton*.

"I ... I need a moment," I tell Riley, darting away before she can stop me.

I hear her say, "She'll be back in just one minute, a slight wardrobe malfunction, I think," as I rush through the doors that lead towards my dressing room. I shut myself in there, grabbing today's designer handbag and fumbling around for Naomi's phone.

She picks up on the second ring.

"Hello?"

"Naomi, we have an emergency."

"Hang on, I just need to ... **OI, ROMAN!** I saw that. You snuck that money under the board! Some banker you are, you're cheating! I saw you!! Someone put Roman's dog piece in prison!"

"**NAOMI!** Walk away from the Monopoly board!" I demand. "I need to talk to you!!"

"I will be back in a bit," I hear her announce, "and I swear, if anyone takes any of my properties, I am going to be VERY angry. Callie, you have my back, right? Sorry . . . Mum or whatever. Keep an eye on your thieving sons!" I hear a door slam. "Hey, Ruby, sorry about that. Honestly, your brothers have no respect for rules. It's maddening."

"I'm aware. Naomi, we have a serious problem," I say, ignoring the ache I get hearing about my brothers.

I usually hate playing board games with my family. Naomi's right, the boys cheat and I come last. Mum tends to get distracted halfway through, and Dad enjoys having the family together so much that he's not really concentrating on the game, he's just cheering us all on no matter what happens. Whenever someone suggests a family board game, I try to get out of it in the hope of being alone in my room to practise my dancing, but they force me to take part. It always descends into a heated argument and someone storming out of the room.

I have no idea why I miss it, but I do.

"What's wrong?" Naomi asks. "Aren't you about to perform live? I tried to get someone to put it on TV, but they won't let me. Your brothers are **NOT** very nice about me or my music. I'd like to see them write a catchy tune when—"

"Naomi, I need you to focus," I interrupt. "I'm about

to do a meet and greet with some competition winners. Ali Carlton is one of them!"

"Who?"

"Ali Carlton! From school!"

"No way."

"YES!"

"Ugh. She is the worst."

"I KNOW! What do I do?"

"What do you mean?"

"I mean, what do I do? I can't speak to her! I can't go out and do the show knowing she's in the audience!"

"Why not?"

"Because . . . she's *Ali Carlton*!" I say in exasperation.

"So?"

"She'll see right through it! She'll see that I'm a fake! She'll laugh at me."

"Ruby, what are you talking about? All she can see in front of her is me. You just have to keep doing what you're doing."

"You don't get it," I say, running a hand through my perfectly styled hair. "She's the most popular girl in school. Look, you can't understand because you're perfect and cool, but I'm not. I'm a loser! A nobody! And people like Ali Carlton—"

"Whoa, whoa, whoa, firstly, take a deep breath,

please," she instructs sternly. "Secondly, I have been walking around as you for almost a week and I can tell you that you are not a nobody."

"Naomi, I appreciate you being nice, but. . ."

"I'm not being nice, Ruby. I'm telling you how it is. You and Alice Carlton—"

"Ali."

"Whatever. You and Ali Carlton are both very talented. You're different in a LOT of ways, but do you know what the main difference between you is? She's not afraid to put herself out there and go for what she wants. Over the last few days, you have proven to yourself just what you can do. You've sung and you've danced in front of thousands of people."

I rest my forehead on the dressing room table, pressing the phone against my ear. "This somehow seems more terrifying."

"You can't let someone like Ali Carlton make you feel like you don't belong up there on that stage. Take it from someone who has been in the business a while – you do."

I smile, hardly daring to believe what I'm hearing. "Thanks."

"Don't thank me yet. I've made a few changes to your life that I'm not sure you'll be thrilled about once we swap back."

"Like what?"

"Nothing you can't handle. You may have a detention or two. But at least I haven't dyed your hair pink, which by the way I still haven't forgiven you for."

"Did Beth see?" I ask eagerly. "What does she think?"

"She thinks it looks stupid."

"No, she doesn't." I laugh. "I was missing her, that's all. Don't worry, it's not permanent."

"If it was, you'd be in BIG trouble." She pauses. "Ruby, how's my mum? Is she OK?"

"Yeah, she's great. She's probably not too happy with me running away from the competition winners, though."

She chuckles. "That sounds about right."

"How about my family? And Beth?"

"Your family are nuts. Same goes for Beth."

"Sounds about right."

There's a moment of silence before she speaks. "Well, I had better get back to the board game. I think I just heard a smash from the sitting room."

"That will be Roman or Reggie knocking over the board in protest. They're not very good losers. I had better get to this meet and greet before the concert starts."

"Good luck, Ruby," she says. "Go show them who you are."

We hang up and, taking a deep breath, I put my

phone away and swing open the door, heading back to the wings where the competition winners are patiently waiting. Riley's expression brightens as I approach with a big smile on my face.

"Thank goodness, you're back," she whispers, before addressing the group. "Here she is! Outfit sorted. Naomi, these are your competition winners and they're very excited to meet you."

"Hi, everyone," I say, waving to them as they all scream and applaud me. "Thanks so much for coming and I really hope you enjoy the show."

"Oh my god, oh my god!" Ali squeals, pushing her way to the front of the group. "PLEASE can we have photos? Can we please?"

The rest of the group looks at me hopefully, all clutching their phones. One of them is so overwhelmed to meet Naomi Starr, he is silently crying.

"Of course."

I smile graciously as they form a jostled queue and Ali passes her phone to Riley, coming to stand next to me.

"You are my favourite pop star in the world – I am your biggest fan," she gushes, flicking her hair back and posing with her hand on her hip.

"Thanks so much, Ali."

She screams, slapping a hand over her mouth. "YOU KNOW MY NAME! **AHHHHHHHHHH!**"

I wince, her scream deafening me temporarily.

"Ah, yeah, my assistant told me your names," I say hurriedly. "Anyway, let's get this photo."

Riley takes the picture and hands back her phone, but before she moves away for the next person to have their photo, she has something more to say.

"Naomi, can I ask you a question?"

"Sure, but we have a few people to get through, so—"

"Do you ever get nervous? Before you go up on stage, I mean?"

I blink at her. "Uh . . . why do you ask?"

"Because I get really nervous. I don't perform in front of huge audiences like you do or anything," she says hurriedly, embarrassed. "But I'm in this small talent show at my school, and every year, I freak out. My singing teacher told me that even pop stars do though, and I was wondering if that was true."

I've never seen Ali like this before. She seems smaller somehow, and the way she's looking at me is so earnest and nervous, like she's allowing herself to be vulnerable. It's the first time I've ever felt like we have something in common.

"It is true," I say, thinking about Riley reeling off

all those times Naomi got stage fright before her big concerts. "I get nervous all the time."

She looks relieved. "That's good to know."

"But you shouldn't let being nervous stop you," I hear myself saying. "You have to find the courage to be yourself and do what you love. Because if you don't, then you'll regret it."

As she's ushered away by Riley so the next person can take their picture, I realize that I wasn't talking to her. Not really.

I was talking to me.

CHAPTER TWENTY-TWO

NAOMI

(AS RUBY)

It's Beth's idea.

She knocks on the door on Sunday night in the middle of a nature documentary Jeroame is making us watch about bees. When he mentioned that he wanted to watch it at dinner, I was like, "**HAHA, YOU'RE A LOSER,**" but now that it's on, I'm completely hooked.

Turns out, bees are cool.

"I've been thinking about the talent show," Beth says, skipping past me and heading straight upstairs to my room.

I follow her, Daisy tripping me up as she bounds up the stairs with us. No matter how hard I try to get rid of her, she won't ever leave me alone when I'm in the house, so now I simply let it happen. She must be weirdly attached to Ruby. I'm getting used to her being at my side all the time and earlier, when I was sitting at the table having dinner, I absent-mindedly put my hand down to stroke her head and had a minor panic when I only felt air and realized she wasn't sitting by my chair as usual.

She was on the other side of me though, so all was well.

"You're here to talk about the talent show?" I ask, watching her climb up on to my bed and make herself comfortable, Daisy following suit. "What is there to talk about?"

"Hello, you got into the final! That's a big deal! We need to talk about what you're going to do for it. We only have a week to rehearse."

"Beth, you interrupted a very fascinating documentary about bees," I tell her, folding my arms. "Do you know how rare it is that I get to sit around and watch documentaries?"

"You watch them all the time," she scoffs, propping up my pillows. "You and Jeroame love them. Last week, you wouldn't stop going on about that documentary you saw on hippos."

"There's one on hippos?" I make a mental note to

ask Simon to download all these shows on my tablet. "Anyway, I already know what I'm doing for the talent show."

"You do?"

"Yeah." I shrug. "Naomi Starr's 'Shining Bright'. I already know the words and choreography, so it's sorted."

She frowns. "Ruby, you can't do the same song that you auditioned with! The judges will have seen it all before."

"So? They loved my performance on Friday. They said it was like watching a real pop star on stage," I remind her smugly.

"Yeah, but you're going to need to up your game to beat Ali. Apparently, she's been working all weekend on her routine. She asked the school caretaker if she could rehearse on the stage and he opened the theatre especially. The only time she had a break was to go see Naomi Starr yesterday." Beth rolls her eyes. "She won a competition to meet her, which is so unfair. We'll never stop hearing about it."

"Fine, I'll pick another of Naomi Starr's songs to perform for the final."

"That won't be enough. We need to do something unique!" She gets her phone out and holds it up so I can see an email on her screen. "I sent this email earlier to the head of music asking if we could book one of the practice rooms every evening after school for the week. We can rehearse there in peace. I think Ali's already booked out the gym hall."

"You want me to rehearse every evening! That's a lot of work."

She looks at me as though I'm mad. "Yeah, but you love it, right? Don't you want to win this thing? You're going to have to work hard, so you can be the best you've ever been on Friday night. I know you've got over your stage fright now, but you can't be complacent."

I'm about to protest when I stop to think about what she's said. It's funny, but she reminded me just then of my mum when we argue about rehearsals. I always thought Mum was nagging and annoying, droning on about my commitments when I knew I didn't need to rehearse because I already knew what I was doing.

But it hits me now that maybe she was trying to do what Beth clearly is – encourage me to be the best I can be.

"All right," I say. "I'll rehearse every night."

"Great. And now I want to tell you about an idea I've had for the show. We have to do something different, right? Because your singing and dancing is great, but Ali is doing the same thing. So, I was thinking about how you can stand out and then I thought about the headmaster's assembly the other day. It inspired me."

"Seriously?" I raise my eyebrows at her. "But his voice is so nasal."

"I was focusing on his words, Ruby." She laughs. "He was talking about the importance of working as a team. It's perfect! It's what we need to win."

"I'm not following you. What do we need?"

"We need a team."

I hesitate. "But ... I'm a solo artist. I mean, Naomi Starr is a solo artist. And I'm performing her songs, so it doesn't make any sense to have a team. Plus, the judges voted me through to the final, not a team."

"You think Naomi Starr is a solo artist?" Beth asks curiously.

"I *know* she's a solo artist!"

She gets a video up on her phone and holds it so we can both see before pressing play. It's a performance of my song "Attention Please" that I did at the Brit Awards last year.

"See?" I point at myself in the spotlight in the middle of the stage. "Performing solo."

"No, she's not. Look at all the dancers around her. Her choreography on its own wouldn't be half as good. It's such a good performance because of everyone on stage, not just one person doing a routine on their own."

I examine the screen, watching in silence until the end of the song. I feel completely thrown. Beth is right! All this time, I thought that the dancers were in the background and it was me that was the main event, but now that I really look, without them I'd look completely ridiculous! The performance would be incomplete. Their dancing complements mine and vice versa.

Oh my God. I've just realized that Martin is a **GENIUS**.

I feel bad now about the time I threw a doughnut at him.

"A team," I say slowly, aware that Beth is watching me. "We need a team. That's how we're going to win. It's brilliant, Beth."

"Why, thank you."

"But how are we going to find people to help us? We only have a week!"

"Don't worry." She grins. "I've got a plan."

As soon as the bell rings signalling the end of Monday, I leap from my seat, excited to get to rehearsals. It's been a while since I've looked forward to a rehearsal so much and I wonder how I managed to lose that feeling.

I wish I could blame it on someone else – Mum, Martin, Simon . . . or is it Sam? But I know that it's all down to me becoming so wrapped up in everything that comes with being a pop star that I kind of forgot why I loved being a pop star in the first place.

"Ruby, a word, please."

My heart sinks as Mr Jones waves me over to his desk before I can escape. I have tried so hard to be on my best behaviour today.

"You can't get detention this week," Beth had warned me the night before. "I don't know why, but the last few days it's like you've gone out of your way to get into trouble. You've never had detention before, but last week you set a record. PLEASE don't waste any of the precious evenings we have to work on this."

As I make my way to the front of the classroom, Beth gives me a pained look.

"I'll meet you in the practice room," she whispers.

I wait until everyone has gone and then sidle up to his desk, reminding myself to be as patient as possible. To be a bit more . . . Ruby.

"Did I do something wrong, Mr Jones?" I ask timidly. "I really can't risk detention this week."

"No, you didn't do anything wrong. In fact, that's what I wanted to say before you left." He finishes wiping the equations off the board and turns to face me. "I'm really pleased with your work today. It seems like you're back on track. Keep it up. That's all I wanted to say."

I'm so shocked, I don't move. "You ... you're pleased with *my* work? My work today?"

"Yes. Your worksheet was completed very well and I could see all your workings clearly."

"Wow! Thank you. I really tried."

"I can tell. See?" He smiles at me. "It pays off when you bother to try."

He starts packing up and I know it's my cue to leave, but I stop in the doorway.

"Uh, Mr Jones, I'm really sorry about last week. I know I was acting out of character and it must have been a bit weird. I was coping with ... a big change and I didn't handle it very well at school."

"That's OK, you don't have to explain anything. We're allowed to have bad days." He picks up his bag and throws it over his shoulder. "In fact, despite everything, it was quite nice to have you speak up a bit more. I don't think you've ever put up your hand in my class, so it's good to see you coming out of your shell. Anyway, enjoy your evening."

It sounds stupid because it was only one lesson on one day, but I feel weirdly proud of myself as I walk away from him. It's nice to know I did well in maths for once.

I get a bit lost in all the corridors but eventually track down the music practice room where Beth is waiting for me, along with about ten other people.

"What did Mr Jones want?" Beth asks, looking concerned.

"To tell me how brilliant I am. Who are all these people?"

"This is your team." She beams at me. "They all want to help you win the talent show. We have four dancers and two backing singers, and everyone else is keen to help with stuff like costume, sound and lighting ... oh! And Ollie is an amazing artist."

"Hang on," I say as Ollie waves at me. "You sit next to me in class. You're always doodling."

"Depending on your song choice, I have some cool ideas for the backdrop set," he tells me excitedly, flicking through his notepad and holding it up to show some cool designs. "Beth mentioned it would be a Naomi Starr song, so I watched a few of her videos at lunch and I got some inspiration. These are all rough sketches, but you get the idea."

"This is amazing!" I turn to Beth. "I can't believe you managed to find a group willing to help us in the space of a *day*!"

"It wasn't that hard. Everyone here is excited to be a part of the show, and it helps that they like you. I told you that you weren't invisible! Did you want to give your ideas for the show first, Ruby? Once we know what you want, we can get going."

"You want *my* ideas for the songs? Really?"

Beth bursts out laughing along with everyone else, apparently finding my stunned reaction hilarious.

"Of course we want your ideas! Why wouldn't we? So" – she glances up at the clock on the wall – "are you ready to start?"

"Absolutely." I clap my hands together. "Let's get to work."

CHAPTER TWENTY-THREE

RUBY

(AS NAOMI)

"Naomi? Time to wake up!"

"Gerroff," I mumble, swatting the air around me.

I hear an "oof" as my hand collides with someone's face, but they don't give up that easy. They prod my shoulder with their finger and their voice is closer to my ear this time.

"Naomi! We're here. You have to wake up."

Disorientated, I pull the eye mask up and blink into the light.

"Where am I? What's happening?" I ask, yawning loudly.

"You're in the back of your limo, which has just

pulled up at the BBC headquarters in Manchester," Riley informs me, reaching into the armrest fridge and pulling out a bottle of sparkling water. "You have three radio interviews before appearing on a morning TV show."

"Oh yeah." I stretch, remembering Sam reeled off this schedule when we left London super early this morning, right before I nodded off. "Why do I have all these interviews again?"

"To promote your new make-up range."

"I have a make-up range. Cool."

"It launched at midnight. Don't worry, though, we've had a team posting about it across social media all through the night."

"That's nice of them."

I take a pocket mirror out of my handbag, hold it up to my face and yelp. My hair is all over the place, now with an eye mask tangled into it, and there's mascara smudged all around my eyes. I was so tired last night that I fell asleep fully clothed face down on the bed without bothering to take off my eye make-up.

I am ruining Naomi Starr's flawless skin.

"I can't promote a make-up range right now!" I cry, attempting to pull the eye mask loose.

"Don't worry, your stylists and beauty team are in the car behind. We came in convoy."

I give up on freeing the eye mask and slump back into the seat.

"Ril— I mean, Mum, can I ask you a question?"

"Do you mind asking the question on the way into the building?" she says, checking her watch and getting out of the car. "We don't want to miss our first radio interview. We're on a very tight schedule today."

"That's actually what my question is about."

I slide out of the car and stretch properly, pleased to see that it's so early and my schedule today has been kept so well under wraps that there are no reporters about to get a photo of me with an eye mask caught in a knot in my hair and make-up all over my face. Naomi would KILL me.

"I was wondering," I continue, falling into step with her, "when do we get some downtime? You know, time to hang out with friends or play board games and stuff."

She looks confused. "Board games?"

"Yeah." I shrug. "It doesn't have to be board games, but don't you ever want to chill for a moment and do something as a family? I feel like I'm always working. There's never any time to sit back and do nothing."

"I can schedule in some time for you to sit back and do nothing, if that's what you're asking. How about Friday at four p.m.," Sam offers, a few steps behind, overhearing our conversation. "Does that work?"

I let out a long sigh, deciding to give up. "Sure. That's great, thank you."

But Riley stops in her tracks and turns to look at me. "What do you mean 'do something as a family'? We're always together, aren't we?"

"Yes, but we're always working," I point out, hoping Naomi won't mind that I'm saying this. "I get that it's important to keep the brand going, and I want to work really hard, but wouldn't it also be fun to sometimes just ... hang out? I feel like we don't ever stop. Ever."

"That's because we don't."

"Right. Look, I love being a pop star, but I'm also a teenager. And you're my manager, but you're also my mum. I don't know, it feels a bit like we're missing out on normal stuff when we don't need to. Does that make sense?"

She starts to nod slowly, taking my words in. "Yes. Yes, it does make sense."

Suddenly, a bunch of paparazzi appear out of nowhere and surround us. I gasp, taken aback by their leaping out right in front of me, and fumble in my bag for sunglasses but I can't find them. My bodyguard jumps into action and puts a protective hand on my back, using his other arm to clear the way in front of us, while Riley flanks the other side. I duck my head, tripping over my shoes as reporters yell a barrage of questions at me.

"*Naomi, are you going for a more laid-back look today?*"; "*Naomi, do you have any comment on the rumours that you fired one of your publicists for wearing the wrong shoes?*"; "*Is it true you're releasing a single inspired by the assistant who betrayed you?*"

We get into the building and I exhale, realizing I was holding my breath that whole time.

"Are you all right?" Riley asks, concerned.

"Yeah. Thank you," I say to the bodyguard, who nods in acknowledgement but stays silent. "I really hate that."

Sam sorts our passes and then a publicist leads the way to the radio studio where I'll be having my interview.

"I'm guessing, Miss Starr, you'll want to pop into a dressing room first to . . . uh" – the publicist searches for the right words – "sort yourself out and prepare for the day of interviews."

I appreciate her tactful way of saying "take your old make-up off, brush your hair and remove the eye mask stuck to your head".

She shows us into a dressing room and, as soon as she's shut the door, Naomi's stylist and beauty team set to work, chatting away about their lives to one another while I sit in silence in the chair, staring at my reflection. Riley leaves to speak to the producers and Sam sits behind me quietly on his iPad.

I miss my boring life. I know it sounds mad, but since the weekend, I've barely had time to think. I have to constantly be on: smiling for cameras, giving all the right responses to important questions, wearing different styles every day and singing perfectly even though I'm exhausted.

Naomi's life is like something out of a fairy tale. I've never felt so happy as when I've been up on stage, singing and dancing to her songs. There's nothing like that adrenaline rush when you come to the end of a song and thousands of people are cheering for you. Everything in her world is beautiful; every room I've walked into has been decorated perfectly and everything she owns is designer, bespoke and unique. It's glamorous and glitzy, and exactly how I'd always imagined it.

But I'm not sure I quite fit into this world.

I miss laughing my head off with Beth. I miss Daisy greeting me every morning like I've been gone for years. I miss my cheery parents, always with their heads in the clouds. I miss my loud, annoying brothers and being able to phone my sister whenever I want.

And I never thought I'd say this, **EVER**, but I kind of miss school.

I miss hanging out with friends, complaining about lessons and teachers together, and the routine of it all.

Plus, I know now that Ali may put on a front, but she sometimes feels as out of place as the rest of us, so I wouldn't be so intimidated by her. Maybe, I'd even try to let her know that I feel the same, in case she needed someone to talk to.

That's what Naomi doesn't have. She's surrounded by people all day long, but has no one to talk to. No one to laugh, complain or dance around stupidly with. I hate the fact that her life is scrutinized by the paparazzi. She has to take herself seriously, because everything she does is taken seriously.

And I feel horrible for her that she felt like she could confide in her previous personal assistant and then they went and sold all those stories to the papers. No wonder she doesn't let anyone in. I wouldn't.

A fear creeps into my mind.

What if this is it? What if Naomi Starr and I can't swap back? We have no idea if living out each other's lives is the answer to this body swap puzzle. It was a guess. Am I never going to be able to spend time with my family again? What about Daisy? Will I never sleep in the same bed as a smelly, perfect scruffball again?

I feel an overwhelming urge to go through **HOW TO SHINE**. The answer *has* to be something to do with that book.

"Sam," I say, swivelling round in my chair as someone wipes away the mascara from under my eyes and someone else attempts to untangle the eye mask from my hair.

He's typing something on the tablet, but snaps his head up immediately.

"Yes?"

"Did you pack my bag for this trip?"

"You stylists packed for you," he says, gesturing to the people by the clothes rail, who are busy pairing shoes with skirts.

"Did anyone pack a book? Kind of old, it was by my bed, I think," I say, remembering seeing it on the bedside table this morning as I got ready in a daze.

The others in the room shake their heads.

"Sam, do we go back to London this afternoon after all these interviews?"

"No, we're in Leeds this afternoon, before heading to Newcastle. We have some promotion spots for this make-up range. And on Thursday night you've got your concert in Birmingham."

"So, I'm not going home any time soon?" I ask, my heart sinking.

"We'll be going home on Friday morning. Is there something you've forgotten?"

"It's a book," I explain, slumping back into my seat. "I left it behind."

"Which book is it?" he asks. "I can download it or we can ask one of the runners here to pop out and buy it for you. There are plenty of book shops around here."

"No, this one you can't find in shops. It's special. You scheduled in some downtime on Friday, right?"

"Yes, that's right," he says proudly, holding up the tablet screen so I can see my hectic, fully booked calendar. "It's scheduled in for four p.m."

"Good. I need to visit a library."

"For this book?" He looks unimpressed. "Are you sure I can't download it for you?"

There's a knock on the door and the publicist who showed us here pops her head round.

"It's time to make your way to the first studio, if you're ready."

"Sure."

I reluctantly push myself up from the chair, my limbs aching from tiredness.

"So, tell me, Sam," I say as enthusiastically as I can muster, "what is it that I am promoting today?"

CHAPTER TWENTY-FOUR

NAOMI

(AS RUBY)

On Friday morning, I come down the stairs with Daisy and hear a voice I don't recognize coming from the kitchen.

"Who took away the lock on the bathroom door? It's so annoying!"

Standing next to Callie is a tall girl in her twenties wearing a hoodie and pyjama shorts. She looks just like Ruby. Daisy barks and scampers over to greet her. Her eyes light up when she sees me standing in the doorway.

"RUBY!" she cries, enveloping me in a huge hug. "I've missed you so much! How's my perfect little sister?"

"Isabella is home for a long weekend," Callie explains,

233

looking like she might burst with happiness. "She got here late last night and didn't want to wake us up. Isn't it great? Such a treat!"

"Mum, the way you're talking, anyone would think I've been away for years." Isabella laughs, pulling away from me and rolling her eyes. "Come on, Ruby, fill me in on your life! How's school? Same as ever? Last time we spoke, you'd just met Naomi Starr in that library! What was she like?"

"Uh ... she was ... a little bit spoilt and rude, actually," I reply honestly. "It's really nice to see you, Isabella."

"You too," she grins, ruffling my hair. "You look taller."

"I was saying that to your dad yesterday," Callie remarks, beaming at us. "I think Ruby has grown the past week. Anyway, both of you come sit down and have breakfast."

Isabella puts her arm round my shoulders and we go to sit down at the table, where the rest of the family are gathered, slowly waking up.

"Roman ate my toast," Reggie says grumpily, as Isabella takes the seat next to him. "Go make me more toast, Roman."

"It was my toast, you stole it from me," Roman argues, yawning with his mouth full. "Make your own toast."

"I'm pretty sure you both stole my toast," John grumbles. "I was the one who put those slices in the toaster and then you two snatched them."

"You're one to talk, John," Jeroame huffs. "I saw you taking a gulp of my coffee."

"Nothing's changed around here, Isabella," Anthony chuckles, passing her the juice.

I clear my throat.

"Actually, I wanted to tell you all something," I begin nervously.

I stay standing, determined to keep their attention. I've worked out that breakfast is less chaotic than dinnertime, so specifically waited until this morning to make the announcement.

"I'm in the final of the school talent show. It's this afternoon at five p.m. And I wondered whether you might want to come and watch me."

Callie and Anthony stop what they're doing and stare at me. Isabella slowly puts the juice down. John and Jeroame look up, intrigued. Roman and Reggie continue eating, but narrow their eyes in exactly the same way as though they don't quite believe me.

"Are you serious?" Isabella asks, looking to her parents for confirmation.

"Yes. I am serious."

I take a deep breath. I really hope Ruby forgives me for what I'm about to do. Although, to be fair, she did dye my hair pink, so it's payback time.

"I never told anyone because I was too nervous, but I love singing and dancing. I'm pretty good at doing both. I've been working really hard on my performance and I auditioned last week and got through to the final."

"Whoa, whoa, whoa." Roman puts down his piece of toast, which Reggie steals from his plate quick as a flash. "Someone said you were in the talent show and I thought it was a joke."

"Yeah, same." John nods. "Are you really going up on stage, Ruby?"

"Yes, and I'd like it if you were all in the audience. If that's possible. I know it's late notice."

"I will be there!" Isabella says firmly. "Ruby, this is **AMAZING** news!! I didn't know you could sing!"

"Neither did I!" Anthony exclaims. "This is fantastic, Ruby. I'll call the hospital and see if someone can cover my shift this afternoon. I am not missing my daughter up on stage in the final of a talent show!"

"Ruby, this is so random!" Jeroame laughs. "It's brilliant; you should have told us about this secret talent of yours. Obviously, we'll be in the audience cheering you on."

"Yeah, you're going to need all the help you can get,"

Roman says with a mischievous smile. Isabella reaches over and whacks him round the head. "**OUCH**. I was joking! I've never been prouder of you, Ruby. If you don't win, those judges will be in serious trouble."

"That's right, Ruby, we've got your back," Reggie says through a mouthful of toast. "This is awesome. We could do with some more talent in this family. I'm holding the fort all on my own."

"I'll go make you your breakfast," John says eagerly, jumping up from the table. "You're going to need your energy today. I can't wait to tell my friends that my little sister made the finals. No pressure, but try to beat that Ali person who usually wins. She keeps giving me evil looks ever since I pointed out a grammar mistake on her party invitation."

"Guys, look at Mum," Isabella insists. "She's crying!"

"I'm not crying," Callie says, sniffing and dabbing at her eyes with her sleeve. "All right, FINE, I'm crying! I'm so proud of you, Ruby! You're amazing!"

I burst out laughing. "You haven't seen me perform yet!"

"I don't have to," she says, her eyes glistening as she smiles up at me. "I already know you're a star. You may have tried to hide that sparkle away, but it's been there all along."

*

I get the text while I am trying to concentrate in history class.

I've been distracted at school all day, too nervous about the talent show to pay attention to any of the teachers.

Ruby's family hasn't made it any easier either. On our way to school, Roman cleared his throat and announced to an entire bus full of students and strangers that his little sister Ruby was in the talent show final and he thought I deserved a big round of applause. Everyone on the bus started clapping and whooping. It was so embarrassing. And awesome.

I even forgave the man squishing me into the bus window with his stupid backpack. Before he got off the bus, he wished me luck, which was nice of him.

Since then, loads of random kids passing me in corridors have shouted, "Good luck, Ruby!" Ruby's brothers have clearly spread the word and it feels like the whole school is behind me.

The talent show is drawing closer and closer, and I am sitting in history class wondering if the Tudors ever felt as nervous as I did. I figure that they probably were quite nervous when they were about to have their heads chopped off or whatever, and just as I am thinking how gross that is, Ruby's phone vibrates with a text.

It's from the library.

This is an automated message reminding you that the book you have on loan is due back TODAY. Please return or renew it by five p.m.

I have the **HOW TO SHINE** book in my bag. The past few days, I've been bringing it to school because some of the chapters have some very handy tips that I've been sharing with the rest of my Starr Squad at the beginning of our after-school rehearsals.

That's what Beth has been calling our talent show team: the Starr Squad, because we're performing a mash-up of two songs from my latest album. The mash-up is SO cool. I wish I could play it for Mum and hear what she thinks.

We've been working so hard all week for the talent show. Beth has been directing and she really has a flair for both the stage vision and also telling everyone what to do. The other dancers have put their all into the rehearsals and I've loved teaching them the choreography to my songs, but also brainstorming ideas with them. At the beginning of the week, they only knew a couple of the steps, and then last night it blew my mind watching them do the whole routine. I couldn't believe how far they'd come in just one week! And that I'd actually taught them all those moves!

Me! Naomi Starr!

Who knew that teaching was one of my many talents?!

Ollie has also done the most incredible job for the backdrop. He worked with the girl who is helping us with lighting, and together they've created an illusion so that for the first part of the song, the backdrop looks like a London alleyway, with graffiti on the buildings lining the street. Then when the mash-up kicks in and we switch to another song, the lighting changes, transforming the backdrop into a pretty, cobbled street with old school lampposts and stars twinkling in the sky above.

"How did you do that?" I'd asked, gasping as we did a technical run-through on the stage.

"Teamwork," Ollie had replied happily.

I'd told him off for being so cheesy, but smiled all the same.

Rehearsing for this talent show has reminded me how much I want to be back in that central London dance studio with my backing dancers and with Martin, no matter how annoying his voice is. It has felt amazing this week to see something come together that I've worked so hard on, and I want to get that feeling with my own music again. I miss being a pop star. It's who I am.

As soon as I read that text, I know I have to go renew **HOW TO SHINE** at the library so Ruby and I can keep working together on swapping back.

"But you have to get ready!" Beth says, when I tell her after school that I have to go out for a bit. She's checking the lens of her camera. John has asked her to photograph the talent show for the school paper. "Do you really have to go somewhere now? We don't have long until it starts!"

"Yes," I say firmly. "But I promise I'll be back in time for the start of the show."

Before she can protest, I turn on my heel and race out of there, the book tucked away safely in my bag. When I get on the bus towards the library, I smile to myself, remembering the last time I was there. It feels like a lifetime ago.

"Ruby!" The librarian gives me a warm smile as I come through the door. "It's so lovely to see you. And I'm about to make your day."

"How?"

"Look who's here again," she whispers, pointing very unsubtly at the arts section. "She walked in about a minute before you did."

A girl steps out from behind the stack of books, clutching a copy of **HOW TO SHINE**.

You know, seeing yourself standing right there in front of you really doesn't get old.

CHAPTER TWENTY-FIVE

RUBY

(AS NAOMI)

"What are you doing here?"

She looks genuinely happy to see me, which is a relief. I thought she might be cross about me almost destroying her make-up empire before it had begun. The pictures of her with mascara smudged round her face and the eye mask tangled in her hair hadn't exactly been great press for launching a beauty line.

Surprisingly, Riley had thought it was a stroke of genius.

"It's all very relatable!" she'd insisted, once she'd finished laughing at the pictures. "No one wakes up with their make-up and hair perfect, do they? I look terrible after a nap, especially in a car. You look remarkably fresh in comparison, trust me."

As Naomi approaches me, Rose looks stunned that we're smiling at each other like old friends. I gesture for Naomi to follow me to a table at the back of the library where we're out of earshot.

"What are *you* doing here?" I ask in response, once we're sitting down.

"I'm here to renew the book. I got the text reminder," she says, watching me closely. "Did you remember off the top of your head that you needed to return your copy today? You're a bigger nerd than I thought."

"I didn't remember." I sit back in my chair, slightly defeated. "It sounds stupid but I thought being here might help me work out how to swap us back. I don't know why."

"It doesn't sound stupid. Everything is worth a try. We got both our copies from here; it makes sense that being in this place might hold the answer somehow."

"I've been hiding in the arts section, flicking through the pages, reading that passage again, hoping that it might glow," I admit. "But it didn't, obviously, because here we are and nothing's changed. I don't know what else to do."

She taps her fingers on the table and I can't help but

smile at the sight of my nails, much longer than they were and beautifully painted. Not one chip in the polish. She may look like me, but it's definitely Naomi.

"Maybe we got it wrong and it's nothing to do with the book," she says eventually. "Maybe it really was nuclear waste."

"You might have been right about that all along." I think back to our meeting in the Ritz when she made that ridiculous suggestion. It feels like a lifetime ago. "It's so crazy that this happened. No one would ever believe us."

"I don't know," she says with a hint of a smile. "We have been acting slightly odd recently. You've definitely got a few more detentions than normal."

"Thanks for that."

"Hey! You weren't the one who had to sit through them. And don't think I didn't notice the eye mask incident." She raises her eyebrows at me. "Was that supposed to be an attempt at accessorizing?"

"It got knotted in my hair by accident," I explain apologetically. "There also wasn't supposed to be any paparazzi around."

"There is ALWAYS paparazzi around."

"I've noticed. How do you cope with that pressure all the time?"

"I was taught how to deal with it from when I was

little. Mum has always protected me and made sure I had a really good security detail." She pauses. "I miss her. I wish I could tell her about all this."

"Why don't we?" I say suddenly. "Why don't we both go to your mum? Or my parents? If we go together and explain everything about the body swap, then they'll see that what we're saying is true!"

She furrows her forehead in concentration, considering my proposal. "But then what?"

"What do you mean?"

"Even if they do believe us, what happens then? I carry on my life but look like you, Ruby, and you carry on your life but looking like Naomi Starr?" She shakes her head. "It wouldn't work. We'd need the whole world to believe us to go back to living our normal lives."

She's right. As soon as she says it, I know she's right.

"So . . . we just keep going as we are?"

"I think that's the only thing we can do."

We sit a few moments in silence and then she gets up, prompting me to do the same. We glumly make our way back through the library.

"Thank you for keeping my career going," Naomi says. "Not many people could have handled it, but you don't seem to be having any trouble."

"I have a lot of trouble with the shoes and constant

outfit changes," I assure her. "Your stylists have had to help me out of a few tight spots when I've got lost in all the weird and wonderful dresses they put me in. After performing in Birmingham last night, I had to go to an awards ceremony and they chose this amazing gown. I put it over my head and the ruffles confused me. I thought I was going to grow old in there."

She giggles. "I miss those dresses! Although, it's been nice not having to worry about what I look like for a couple of weeks. Kind of like being on holiday."

"So, you haven't even tried? The least you could do whilst parading around as me is give me some style points. You won teen fashion icon of the year! I know because I accepted that award the other day."

"Hey, you should be grateful that I haven't got you expelled," she says proudly, as though it's some great achievement. "Although, there have been a couple of close calls. Your school file is now much more impressive. Did you know that it's against the rules to trip people up in PE? So much for competitive spirit."

"Oh no," I groan. "I've managed to go happily unnoticed for years."

"What's so wrong with standing out?" she asks curiously.

Rose clears her throat as we shuffle closer to her

desk. "Did you want to renew that book, Ruby? And uh … Naomi Starr, I don't know if you remember, but you also took a copy. I must admit I wasn't expecting to see you here ever again. I assumed that book might be lost for ever."

"Yes, I'm sorry for snatching it out of Ruby's hands so rudely," I say pointedly, as Naomi rolls her eyes. "Your library is a wonderful haven of imagination and I respect that."

Naomi pretends to retch. Rose looks at me, bewildered.

"Also," I continue, because of the eye-rolling and retching and also because it's quite fun to have this kind of power, "I would like to donate some money towards this much-deserving library. It's really the least I can do for my appalling behaviour last time I was here."

"How generous of you!" Rose exclaims.

"Yes. How generous of you," Naomi says through gritted teeth.

"You are very welcome. Maybe I'll write some songs about this place," I add wistfully, for effect.

"Maybe I'll give Daisy back to the rescue centre where I got her," Naomi says. "She's been very annoying recently."

"WHAT? DON"T YOU—" I stop myself as she grins

triumphantly. I cough, lowering my voice to a mumble. "Anyway, the point is I'd like to renew the book."

"Me too," Naomi says.

"Ah, well that won't be a problem for you, Ruby," Rose says, typing into her computer, before looking up at me. "The only thing is Naomi, you need to be a registered member of the library to borrow a book. But as you're donating so generously to the library, I imagine you won't mind taking the time to fill out a form!"

"No problem," I say cheerily, taking the form she slides across from me and clicking my pen at the ready. "How fun to be a member of such a great library."

"Yes, how fun to give out all your personal details to a member of the public," Naomi says sarcastically. "Because that's what all famous pop stars do."

I pause at the bit asking for a phone number, taking her point.

"Perhaps," Naomi continues, smiling sweetly at Rose, "on this occasion, you could let Naomi Starr be a member without needing all this information? Especially as she's giving so . . . generously to the library. You can put down *my* information under her registration."

"Of course, I completely understand." She types away at the keyboard. "There you go, all sorted. You can borrow that book now. But don't return it late!" She laughs,

248

waggling her finger at me. "I wouldn't want to fine Ruby on your behalf. Enjoy the books!"

"You were joking about Daisy, right?" I say as soon as we're outside. "You were joking. Just confirm you were joking!"

"I was joking," she says calmly, checking my phone. "Once you get past her stinky breath and scruffy appearance, she's not too bad. Right, I have to go. There's a bus coming along in a minute and I'm going to be late."

"Late for what? It's a Friday. Ooh! Is there a nature documentary on tonight that you guys are watching?"

"There's your car," she says, nodding at the limo parked down the road. "What do you have on this evening?"

"A party. I can't remember if it's mine or someone else's," I say, watching as the car pulls up alongside us. "But I do know that it's important to be there. I'll see you soon; keep texting."

One of the security team has jumped out the car and is waiting, holding the door open for me. Before I get in, Naomi stops me.

"Hey. Can I just say something?" She takes my arm, pulling us out of earshot. "I know that we want to swap back now, but I'm glad that this happened in the first place. This experience has really opened my eyes. Your world is pretty cool. In its own way."

"Thanks." I smile at her. "Same for you."

She cranes her neck, looking over my shoulder. "There's the bus. I better go. See you soon, Ruby."

She dashes across the road to get to the bus stop in time and it's not until I'm in the car, driving to the party that I realize she got on a bus going in the wrong direction to home.

Why would she be heading back to school?

CHAPTER TWENTY-SIX

NAOMI

(AS RUBY)

"There you are!"

Beth pounces on me as soon as I walk into the green room, which is actually just a classroom that Mrs Jennings has declared to be the room for her "artists" to get ready before the show.

"We're about to do a huddle," Beth informs me, putting her arm over my shoulders. "Come on, Starr Squad, everyone come in together."

"You waited for me to do the huddle? Thanks!"

"Duh!" She shakes her head as though I've just said something stupid.

I wish I could tell her that I've performed to audiences

of thousands and I've never once been invited to join a huddle beforehand. Not that I can blame my dancers or crew. I've never even bothered to ask them their names.

"Ruby, do you want to say something?" Beth asks, as our team gathers and links together in a circle.

"Actually, I do." I clear my throat. "Even if this show is a disaster, even if I fall over flat on my face, forget the words or forget how to dance, I've had the best time putting this performance together with you all. I've often felt like I'm on the sidelines, but this week I didn't. Thanks so much for letting me be a part of your team."

"Very cute." Beth grins. "But try not to fall flat on your face, forget the words or forget how to dance. Let's smash this."

Everyone laughs and we break apart to high-five each other before Mrs Jennings comes into the green room and calls Ali's name. She's up first.

"Hey, Ali," I call out as she gets to the door. "Good luck."

She stops and, for a moment, I think she might turn round and thank me, but she thinks better of it and, holding her chin up high, swans out of the room.

"Aren't you coming to watch?" Beth asks, as I take a seat. "We're going to go stand in the wings and check out the competition."

"I'll be there in a moment. I want to get myself ready."

When my team and the other finalists have filed out the room, I take deep breaths in and out, shaking out my hands, trying to ignore the butterflies flitting about in my stomach. All I want is Mum to be here, giving me one of her pep talks. When I'm in the wings before a big concert, holding the microphone, listening to the crowd chant as they wait for my entrance, she always comes to stand next to me.

"You can do this," she usually says, squeezing my hand. "Remember, you're doing what you love."

I wish I could tell her how much I appreciate her saying stuff like that. I've never even thanked her.

I reach to get **HOW TO SHINE** out of my bag. Mum's not here but this book has some good words of advice to calm my nerves. My hands are so clammy that as I get the book out, I drop it and it falls to the floor.

I pick it up and as I plonk it on to my lap it falls open on a familiar page:

Sometimes, to learn about yourself, you need a different view. Step into someone else's shoes, tread in their footsteps, see things through their eyes.

See how you shine.

"Trust me," I say out loud, "I've been there, done that."

At first, I think I'm imagining it but then it gets clearer and brighter. *The book is glowing.*

OH MY GOD THE BOOK IS GLOWING! **THE BOOK IS GLOWING!**

"No, wait, not now! Ruby is meant to be on stage any min—"

WHOOOOOOOOOOOOOOOSH!!

CHAPTER TWENTY-SEVEN

RUBY

(AS NAOMI)

I find a deserted table in the back corner of the party, so I can have a moment to myself.

I have been informed by Sam that I'm at an album launch of a singer-songwriter who I apparently don't like very much.

"Then why am I here?" I asked Sam under my breath after giving the hostess two air kisses and moving into the crowd.

"Because you said it was one of those events that it was important to be seen at," he explained, checking my schedule for where we were supposed to be going afterwards. "Your mum and Martin should be here somewhere."

When we couldn't find them, Sam had disappeared

to get me a sparkling elderflower – they were serving sparkling pomegranate, which according to him wasn't what I wanted – and I scanned the room for a secluded spot to hide in.

I sit down and, after people-watching for a bit, wondering how everyone in this room was so impossibly glamorous, I get **HOW TO SHINE** out of my bag. I'm so bored; I'd much rather be reading. I accidentally drop the book and hurry to get it up from the floor, worried that I've scuffed the pages.

As I pull it up on to my lap, it falls open on to a page I know off by heart:

> *Sometimes, to learn about yourself, you need a different view. Step into someone else's shoes, tread in their footsteps, see things through their eyes.*
> *See how you shine.*

"Trust me," I mutter, reading it through and smiling to myself, "I have taken your advice."

Wait a second … is it … is it GLOWING? THE BOOK IS GLOWING!

FINALLY!

WHOOOOOOOOOOOOOOOSH!!

CHAPTER TWENTY-EIGHT

NAOMI

Someone is prodding my arm. Hard.

"Really, Naomi," a voice says in that weary tone I've missed so much, "you've fallen asleep at someone's party! With your mouth open and everything."

It worked. *It worked*!

I'M BACK!

"MUM!" I shriek, blinking away my blurred vision to see her frowning at me.

I jump up and wrap my arms around her, hugging her so tight and with such force that she stumbles backwards.

"Hey, Mum," I say, tears running down my face as she hugs me back. "I've missed you."

"What?" She laughs. "I saw you about two hours ago at our perfume meeting."

"I know," I say, pulling away and looking up at her. "But it felt like weeks."

"That's very sweet of you. Are you all right?" Her eyebrows knit together in concern as she examines my face. "Why are you crying? What's going on?"

"I'm crying because I'm happy! Because I'm **ME!** I am me, right? I am Naomi Starr? WHO HAS A MIRROR IN HERE?"

Mum reaches into her handbag and passes me her compact mirror. I open it and, on seeing my reflection, I scream in joy and start dancing on the spot.

"I'm ME! That's right! I'm me! Wooooooo!" I chant, launching into a spontaneous dance routine around the table. "WHAT A TIME TO BE ALIVE!"

Mum is staring at me, her eyes as wide as saucers.

"Well, yes, you are you," she says, baffled. "And you're great."

"I'm so happy to be me! And SIMON! No . . . wait . . . SAM! There you are, Sam!" I exclaim, grabbing his hand and jumping up and down on the spot. "Your name is Sam, not Simon. Of course it's Sam! You look like a Sam! I will never get your name wrong again because I appreciate you and all the work you do. It's so good to see you!"

"It's great to see you, too," he replies, looking a little

scared by my outburst. "I brought you your sparkling elderflower."

"My favourite drink! You are the **BEST!**"

"What's going on?" Martin says, appearing behind Mum. "There's a lot of noise coming from over here."

"MARTIN! OMG, EVERYBODY, IT'S MARTIN!" I clap my hands together, making everyone jump. "Martin, I've missed you and your ridiculous voice!"

"Excuse me?"

"Martin, we have SO much to talk about. Mainly, I want to tell you how excited I am to rehearse with you again. We are going to make our shows bigger and better, and I want to tell you now that I will be completely dedicated. I will be on time and I will work harder than ever before. You, my friend, are a genius choreographer. I don't say that enough."

Martin's face lights up at my words. I've never seen him so happy.

"Thank you, Naomi. That means a lot."

"No, thank **YOU!** Thanks to all of you, my brilliant team!" I turn back to Mum and give her another hug. "I am so happy to be home!"

"You're not at home, darling, we're at a party," she says, glancing around as people start to stare. "Are you sure everything's all right?"

"Mum, everything is brilliant and exactly how it should be and ... wait, what time is it?"

I look around for a handbag and spot one of my designer bags sitting next to my seat. As IF Ruby put my handbags on the floor. She has so much to learn.

I dig around in it and pull out my phone triumphantly.

"Hello, phone! My beautiful, precious phone!" I press it against my cheek affectionately. "I've missed you!"

Mum and Martin share a look.

I should rein it in.

"Ali's set will be finishing up by now! WE HAVE TO GO!" I yell, grabbing my handbag and then Mum's hand, dragging her through the party and towards the door.

"Wait, Naomi! You're pulling my arm off!" Mum gasps. "What is going on?"

"A friend needs me right now. A *real* friend."

"Who?"

"I'll explain another time." I turn to Sam who, as always, appears by my side. "Is Kelly waiting with the car somewhere?"

"She's parked down the road," he replies, typing into his phone. "I'll get her to bring the car to the front now."

"Thank you, Sam."

"Naomi, can you tell me what all the fuss is about? You're acting so strangely!"

"Honestly, Mum, you wouldn't believe me if I told you." I laugh, fishing a pair of sunglasses out from my bag in preparation. "Let's just say that recently I had the chance to walk in someone else's shoes and it made me realize a few things. Like, how lucky I am to have such a supportive, understanding family, and how we really need to sit down properly and come to a compromise on scheduling, because we should be having some downtime together, as well as working so hard, and—"

She holds up her hand to stop me from going on. "I know. I've been thinking about this ever since you brought it up in Manchester. We *should* have some more time as a family. You're absolutely right."

"I am?" I say, surprised that she's agreed with me so easily.

"Yes." She smiles and takes a deep breath. "Look, it's important to me that you succeed in what you want to do, but it's much more important that, in whatever you do, you're happy. I spent most of my life terrified that if I didn't work hard enough, my career would slip away, and recently I've forgotten that you're not living *my* career, you're living yours. And I have a feeling that no matter what, you're going to be just fine. You're the biggest star I know."

I beam up at her. "Wow. Thanks, Mum. To be fair, I learnt from the best."

She laughs, putting an arm round me and squeezing me close. "Tomorrow, let's talk about scheduling in some downtime at least once a week. I can't even remember how to play most board games. I'd like to learn again."

"Your car is here," Sam announces, as a member of my security team comes through the doors, ready to escort me back out.

"Show time!" I squeal, putting on my sunglasses. "I have MISSED this!"

The doors fling open and as soon as I step out, the camera flashes of the photographers lined against the roped-off red carpet start going off like crazy.

"**HELLO, LONDON!**" I cry, waving at the photographers. "It is good to be back!"

Kelly is waiting by the limo and I squeal when I see her.

"Hey, Kelly! Thanks so much for bringing the car round. I have SO many bus stories to tell you," I inform her, chuckling at her puzzled expression as I slide on to the leather seats. I quickly pull up the armrest to check my bottles of sparkling water are all still there. "Oh, car! I'm so lucky to have you and your clever refrigerator unit! Mum, sit next to me!"

"Where are we going, Miss Starr?" Kelly asks, once

Mum, Sam and the bodyguard have climbed in and taken their seats down the side of the limo.

"To Hartfell School, please. As soon as possible."

"A school? Why on earth are we going to a school? Who is this friend of yours?" Mum asks curiously.

"Her name is Ruby. And she's about to perform in her school talent show."

"Hang on, are you talking about that girl who interrupted our brunch at the Ritz last week? The one for whom I paid that taxi fare?"

"Oh yeah, but don't hold that against her, she wasn't herself at the time."

"This school talent show isn't in your schedule," Sam points out, looking panicked as he scrolls through his beloved iPad.

"We're going off schedule tonight, Sam. It's important that we're in the audience for this."

"But *why*?"

"Because she's my friend and she needs me," I say firmly, typing out a text. "I want to be there for her."

"Then we'll make sure you're there," Mum says, giving Kelly a nod. "How do you know this Ruby person?"

I look up from my phone and shoot her a grin. "It's a long story."

CHAPTER TWENTY-NINE

RUBY

Someone is shaking me awake.

"Ruby? Ruby! Wake up!"

I rub my eyes, disorientated, and open them to see Beth staring at me.

"*Beth*?" I whisper, my mouth dry. "BETH!"

I scream at the top of my lungs and jump to my feet to give her the biggest hug in the world.

"It's you! It's really you! Am I me? **AM I?**"

"Um ... what are you talking about, you weirdo?" she laughs, squiggling out of my tight grip. "Did you have a nightmare or something? How did you fall asleep so quickly?"

"It is so good to see you! Wait, I need a mirror! Do you have one?"

"Sure, hang on."

She wanders over to her backpack, tucked under one of the desks in the classroom we're in, and gets out a small compact mirror, holding it up for me. I scream when I look at my reflection, before pulling her in for another gigantic hug, jumping up and down excitedly as I do.

"What is going on?" she asks, giggling.

"I'm so happy to see you," I gush, pulling away and looking at her. "You are the best, most brilliant friend in the whole world. Did you know that? And I am so lucky to have you in my life. Thank you for always being there for me."

"Uh, you're welcome?" She gives me a strange look. "What's brought this all on? Is this some form of stage fright or pre-show nerves?"

"Ha! Why would I have stage fright or pre-show nerves? I'm **RUBY!** I'm me!" I dance around the classroom excitedly. "I can't believe it! I'm home!"

"You see school as home?" She wrinkles her nose. "That's weird."

"Hang on." I stop dancing. "Why are we at school? Isn't it Friday night?"

"Is this a joke? Are you joking right now?" Beth puts her hands on her hips. "We don't really have time for this, Ruby. Ali has finished her performance and that magician guy has just come off stage. The string quartet or whatever are on now, and we're going on stage after them. So, come on, let's get backstage."

"Backstage?" I repeat slowly, checking her mirror again that it is me and I'm not still Naomi Starr. "That doesn't make any sense. Why would I need to go backstage?"

"In order to walk *on* stage for the talent show final."

Wait. Did she say . . . the *talent show final*?

"I just need to check my phone," I croak, scanning the room for my bag and finding it under a chair.

There are a slew of texts waiting for me.

IT WORKED! THE MAGIC WORKED!
I'M NAOMI AGAIN! YOU'RE RUBY
AGAIN! WE SWAPPED BACK!
WOOOOOOOOOOOOOOOO!!!!!!

HOW CRAZY IS THIS?! I wonder why
it suddenly worked?

Oh, by the way, any second now
you're about to go on stage in the
school talent show final

**Probably should have mentioned
that earlier**

"I'm in the school talent show final," I say, reading her messages with horror.

"That's right, keep saying it!" Beth says cheerily. "Now, let's go backstage and get ready!"

Before I can kick my brain into action, Beth has grabbed my arm and is leading me out of the classroom and towards the stage doors of the school theatre. I begin to panic. I have no idea what I'm doing. There's no way I can go out on stage and perform as *me*. I don't know whether I can do this! This is all WAY too overwhelming!

My phone vibrates in my hand.

You're singing two of my songs as
a mash-up. Don't worry, you'll know
when to switch because the music
changes up. The songs are 'Attention
Please' and 'My Own Way'. I've seen
you perform both of those in the past
week so I KNOW YOU CAN DO IT.
The choreography is exactly the same,
and you have a team on stage with

you. They're awesome, go with it.

Good luck!!

I am going to kill her.

My phone goes again.

P.S. I invited your whole family to

watch.

Hope you don't mind.

NOW I'M REALLY GOING TO KILL HER.

"My *family* is here," I squeak, a lump building in my throat.

"Yeah, all of them. I saw them in the audience when I peered through the curtains earlier," Beth tells me happily. "Your parents, all your brothers and even Isabella. They're so proud of you. Roman and Reggie spent lunch break making you a banner."

"They . . . they did?"

"Yeah. To be honest with you, they're not the most artistic. There's glitter everywhere and they've drawn a load of stick people around the "Go Ruby", and I think the stick people are supposed to be smiling, but their faces look super creepy. It looks like a toddler has done it. Still, it's sweet that they tried."

"Yeah, it is," I reply, stunned that they have made so much effort for me.

"OK," Beth says, grabbing my shoulders. "I have to go out to the audience to take photos for the paper. Everyone else is waiting backstage."

There's an eruption of applause from the theatre as the string quartet comes to a finish and Beth gives me a quick hug, before pulling away and checking her camera.

"That's my cue! I'll see you on the other side!"

"B-but. . ."

"Go, Starr Squad!"

She sprints down the corridor and round a corner, leaving me standing alone by the stage door. My whole body feels numb, while my brain goes into overdrive imagining all the things that might happen if I take the steps to go backstage. I might fall on my face in front of the **WHOLE SCHOOL**. I might sing out of tune, forget the words, ruin the whole show for everyone. And this time I can't hide behind Naomi Starr. This time, I'm me, Ruby.

"I don't think I can do this," I whisper into the empty corridor.

My phone vibrates. It's Naomi again.

I imagine you're freaking out about now. But we both know that it's time

for you to shine in your own right. Isn't

that what the book has been telling

you all along?

I read her message through three times. I really wish she wasn't making any sense, but she is. Because as well as feeling sick with nerves right now, I also feel a rush of excitement to have the chance to be on stage singing and dancing in front of an audience again.

I remember Riley Starr telling me to pretend I'm messing about, dancing around my bedroom, doing what I love.

"Ah, Ruby, you're here," Mrs Jennings says, opening the stage door to find me right in front of her. "Come on, you're next. I'm about to announce you. Are you ready?"

I take a deep breath.

"Yes." I nod, following her into the wings. "I'm ready."

A group of my classmates are waiting for me backstage and as I approach them, their faces light up with excitement. This must be the rest of my group. One of them passes me a microphone, telling me not to turn it on until we're in our starting position on stage.

"Remind me what the starting position is again?" I ask innocently.

"Good one," she whispers, giggling.

Oh well. It was worth a try. Let's just hope it's obvious.

The crowd erupts into applause and cheers when Mrs Jennings announces my name as the next act. She walks off stage, wishes us luck and then we are ushered on as the lights go down. Remembering that Naomi said the first song of the mash up was "Attention Please", I stand in the middle of the stage with my head down, microphone at the ready, just as Naomi does in all her performances of that one. Just as I've done for the past two weeks.

The other dancers take their places around me and don't say anything, so it looks like I've done the right thing. Phew.

The crowd falls silent. A spotlight shines down.

The intro of the song begins. I lift my head, hold up the microphone and I start to sing, launching into the first steps of the dance.

I really thought that nothing could beat that feeling of being Naomi Starr, performing to all her fans. But I was wrong. As I dance around the stage, singing two of my favourite songs, watching the crowd get to their feet and start dancing and clapping along, I have never been happier. I forget that everyone is watching. I forget to be nervous and scared of what they might think.

I'm just doing what I love.

I get to the end of the song and strike the finishing pose on the last beat, throwing my head back and punching the air. The theatre explodes with noise. It's an overwhelming reaction. Everyone is clapping and cheering, and we get a standing ovation. I feel in a daze as the other dancers on stage pounce on me, huddling together to jump up and down, screaming, "We did it! We did it!"

They then form a line with me in the middle so that we can bow together.

The lights have come up over the audience and I can see my family taking up the majority of the first row. Mum and Dad are both crying tears of joy, Isabella is blowing me kisses and the boys are going bonkers, whooping and chanting, "**RUBY TO WIN! RUBY TO WIN!**"

We take a second bow and I smile at Beth, who is standing amongst the audience taking pictures. She lowers her camera for a moment to grin back at me.

Just before I walk off stage, the applause from the audience still going strong, I notice someone standing right at the back, hiding in the shadows. She's wearing designer sunglasses and is standing with a tall woman who is on her phone, a man who is nervously typing something on a tablet, and a stern-looking security guy, who is checking his earpiece.

Catching my eye, she gives me a small nod before whispering something to her bodyguard.

He pushes open the door behind her and, just like that, she's gone.

EPILOGUE

NAOMI

A WEEK LATER

I spot her sitting on a bench behind the library.

She's holding Daisy's lead as she strains to chase a pigeon hopping about nearby. I chuckle to myself as I walk towards them, enjoying the freedom of no security and no paparazzi.

"Hey," I say, sitting down next to her on the bench.

"Hey!" she replies, brightening. "You made it."

Daisy jumps up at me and I burst out laughing as she slobbers all over my face, Ruby desperately trying to pull her back.

"I've missed you, you big scruffball," I say, giving her a good scratch behind the ears. "Do you think she recognizes me at all? Or does she greet everyone like this?"

"I think she knows," Ruby says, getting a treat out of her bag so she'll leave me alone. "Dogs can sense stuff."

She attempts to make her sit before giving her the treat, but Daisy snatches it from her hand and munches it happily.

"How did you get here without the paparazzi noticing?" she asks, holding on to Daisy tightly as she gets back to focusing on the pigeon.

"I tweeted that I was on my way to go shopping in Westfield, then asked Kelly to drive there and back in my car. Hopefully, that will fool the press for long enough."

"Nicely played." She leans back on the bench. "You returned the book, then?"

"Yeah. You?"

She nods. "It felt weird handing it back. Like nothing had ever happened and it was a normal book, nothing special about it."

"I know what you mean. When you suggested we return our copies today, part of me wanted to say no and hold on to it for ever," I admit. "I think I could have got away with it, too. The librarian was genuinely shocked to see me again. I don't know why, since thanks to you, I'm now an official member and I've pledged a lot of money to this place."

"It's a great cause." She laughs. "I've never seen Rose happier than when I said that."

"Yeah, well, this library means a lot to me, anyway. Do you think Rose has any idea of what those books can do? Do you think she knows about their . . . magic?"

"No, I don't. I hinted around that and it went straight over her head. She talked about how it helped her when she had to do a presentation for a librarian conference and was nervous about public speaking. She didn't seem too upset that you might not return that other copy either. I think she has no idea just how special those books are."

"Probably a good thing."

"Probably."

Daisy paws at Ruby's leg and she gives her another treat. She gobbles it up, keeping an eye on the pigeon at all times.

"So," I nudge her arm, "how's life after winning the school talent show? Are you mobbed by fans in the corridors?"

She bursts out laughing. "Not exactly. But I don't feel so invisible any more, which is scary sometimes but also a good thing, I think. The day after the talent show, Mum and Dad put together a list of all these prestigious music holiday camps around the country. They want me to apply to all of them! They're being so encouraging and supportive. I don't know why I didn't tell them about my singing and dancing sooner."

"Ruby, that's great news. You should definitely apply! And hey, tell me which camp is top of your list and if you want, I can put in a good word."

"Thanks, but that's OK. I want to do this on my own. I think I can."

"I *know* you can." I adjust my sunglasses. "And how is my good friend, Ali Carlton, doing? When you messaged saying you'd won the talent show, I wondered how she'd taken the news."

"Actually, she was OK with it," Ruby says with a knowing smile. "After the show, John told her that he wanted to do a profile on all the finalists for the school paper and she cared much more about that. She even congratulated me on my performance and invited me to her party the next day."

"You're joking! Did you go?"

She shakes her head. "I decided I'd much rather stay in and watch a programme on polar bears with Beth. We ate way too much ice cream and she made me laugh my head off with her teacher impressions. She's so good at them."

"She really is."

Daisy gets bored of pigeon-watching and trots over to me, sitting at my feet and resting her head on my lap.

"I read rumours online that you're adding another London date. If there are any tickets going spare, maybe you could let me know," Ruby says hopefully.

"I'll think about it," I tease. "It's in a month and we're coming up with a brand new show. Martin and I have been working all week on our vision."

She looks confused. "You're working together?"

"Yes, we are. I've shown complete dedication this week and it's paying off; he's involving me much more in the creative side of the process. I think he's forgiven me for my previous skipping out on rehearsals and ... ahem ... claiming I was allergic to his scent."

She grimaces. "My bad. Sorry about that. How is your mum? And Sam?"

"Sam is on holiday. I figured he could use a break." I reach into my bag and pull out a bottle of water, unscrewing the cap and taking a sip. "And Mum is good. We chatted about my schedule issues and came to a happy compromise. I took notes from your family actually."

"Seriously?" She looks impressed. "Like what?"

"When we had some time off earlier this week, we

278

played Monopoly. It was so nice to see her relax for once. I also invited Martin, Kelly, my chef and all of my dance crew to join us. It got very out of hand. We discovered that Chef is a dirty cheat and Martin can be a real diva."

Ruby throws her head back and laughs. "That is brilliant."

"But my biggest piece of news is that I'm launching the Starr Scholarship," I say excitedly, unable to keep it from her any longer. "It was my idea and Mum has set up meetings to make it happen. It's a full scholarship to a top London performing arts school for an outstanding musician. I want to give others an opportunity to see the world from my point of view. What do you think? Do you like the idea?"

"Naomi, I think it's **AMAZING!**" she exclaims, beaming at me.

"Oh good. I told Mum that I needed to check it with you first."

Her forehead creases in confusion. "Why would you need to check it with me?"

"Because when big things happen in your life, you're supposed to tell your friends, right?"

"Right."

We sit quietly for a moment, watching the pigeons. I stroke Daisy's head happily.

"Hey," Ruby says suddenly, breaking the silence, "if you're free on Saturday, would you like to come to my house for a sleepover? Beth is coming and it would be nice for you to meet her properly, as you. She might have a minor heart attack when you walk in, but I reckon you're used to dealing with that reaction."

I blink at her, taken aback. "Really? You're inviting me for a sleepover?"

"Yeah. I know you're famous and everything, but this is a SUPER exclusive invitation. Only *best* friends allowed." She flashes me a grin. "You can let me know once you've checked your schedule if you like."

"For such a one-of-a-kind invitation? No need to check." I smile back at her so widely, my jaw hurts. "I'll be there."

ACKNOWLEDGEMENTS

I'm super excited to create a brand new book! I feel very lucky to be a part of such a fun project. Thank you to everyone at Scholastic for making this happen: your hard work and dedication as a company is so inspiring. Lauren Fortune, Aimee Stewart, Mary Jones, Penelope Daukes, Clare Hennessey, Kate Graham: thank you so much for everything you have done, I appreciate every single one of you.

Thank you to Nuno Ramalhão for the cover art.

Katy Birchall, once again it's fantastic to collaborate with you. One of the most talented multi-taskers I know! Thank you for your brilliance and for bringing **STAR SWITCH** to life!

Thank you to my super cool agent, Lauren Gardner, for your support and knowledge: you are amazing!

To all my friends and family, thank you for reading my books... or pretending too! Haha! Ruby, I know you have :) Thank you for your continued support.

To all the readers, I hope you enjoy **STAR SWITCH**! Continue to shine, be kind to one another and go for your dreams!

All my love

ALESHA

X

Photo by John Wright

ALESHA DIXON first found fame as part of Brit-nominated and Mobo Award-winning group Mis-teeq, which achieved 2 platinum albums and 7 top ten hits, before going on to become a platinum-selling solo artist in her own right. Alesha's appearance on *Strictly Come Dancing* in 2007 led to her winning the series and becoming a judge for three seasons.

Since then she has presented and hosted many TV shows including CBBC dance show *Alesha's Street Dance Stars, Children In Need, Sport Relief* and BBC1's *The Greatest Dancer*. She is a hugely popular judge on *Britain's Got Talent*.

Alesha and Katy Birchall also collaborated on the smash hit **LIGHTNING GIRL** series: the first book was the biggest-selling middle grade debut of 2018.

Photo by Aimee Stewart

KATY BIRCHALL is the author of the side-splittingly funny *The It Girl: Superstar Geek*, *The It Girl: Team Awkward*, *The It Girl: Don't Tell the Bridesmaid* and the *Hotel Royale* series, *Secrets of a Teenage Heiress* and *Dramas of a Teenage Heiress*. Katy also works as a freelance journalist and has written a non-fiction book, *How to be a Princess: Real-Life Fairy Tales for Modern Heroines*.

Katy won the 24/7 Theatre Festival Award for Most Promising New Comedy Writer with her very serious play about a ninja monkey at a dinner party.

When she isn't busy writing, she is reading biopics of Jane Austen, daydreaming about being an elf in *The Lord of the Rings*, or running across a park chasing her rescue dog, Bono, as he chases his arch nemesis: squirrels.

Look out for Katy's brand new series, also out now:

No one ever warned me that when you get angry, bright sparks might explode from your fingertips.

But that's exactly what happened. One minute I was watching some school bullies round on my little sister in the playground, and the next minute my hands went all hot and tingly and suddenly these beams of light came flying out from my palms, like a lightning storm.

I think I scared myself more than anyone

else. No one actually saw where the sparks came from, just a flash of blinding light behind them, and then when they turned around, there I was staring wide-eyed at my hands and madly wiggling my fingers.

One of the girls snorted as she watched me bring my hand right up to my face, so it was almost touching the end of my nose, and examine my little finger closely.

"Isn't that your older sister, Clara?" she sneered. "What on earth is she doing?"

"She's as odd as you are!" sniggered another one, as they all looked me up and down. I gulped.

Getting them to pick on me instead of Clara wasn't technically my original plan. I figured I would just tell them to leave her alone, rather than distract them by becoming a human firework. Still, they weren't interested in Clara any more and it seemed that they weren't all that curious about a random and inexplicable burst of light in the middle of the playground either.

So that was something.

"What do you want, Aurora?" a tall boy said to me, raising his eyebrows.

"U-um..." I stammered, my hands still held up in front of my face. "I was just, uh, looking at my ... scar."

I held out my left hand, so they could see the swirled scar across my palm.

"I was born with it. Weird, isn't it? Scars appear when the skin tissue heals over a wound to protect and strengthen it. Interesting. Right?"

This was not my proudest moment.

Clara looked at me as though I had lost my mind. I tried to think of something else to say, something a bit more impressive than healing-skin-tissue facts, but I was still a bit in shock from shooting light beams out of my hands. It had never happened before. The ringleaders glanced at each other in confusion. The tall one opened his mouth to speak but luckily the bell rang sharply, signalling break-time was over.

"Saved by the bell! Come on, Clara. See you lot later – fun talking to you!" I laughed nervously, as Clara darted round them to stand next to me. I threw my arm round her and hurriedly dragged her towards the school building before they could say anything else.

Kizzy found it hilarious. I decided not to tell her about the whole sparks-coming-out-of-my-hands thing because I didn't want her thinking her best friend was weird, but I needn't have worried. She knew I was weird.

"Healing skin tissue?" she giggled, getting her favourite pen out from her pencil case and opening her notebook as we waited for Mrs Damsel to start our health class.

"It was the first thing I could think of," I sighed, looking accusingly at my palm as though it was my scar's fault that I'd said something so silly. "They'll never let me live it down. I think one of them is in gymnastics club with Suzie Bravo, so I bet they'll tell her all about it."

Kizzy and I glanced across to where Suzie was sitting with Georgie Taylor. Georgie was showing Suzie her cool new backpack, which was black and covered in all these small neon flowers. I just knew it was the latest must-have accessory. Georgie was the trendiest person in our year, maybe even in the entire school,

thanks to her mum who was in charge of publicity for loads of big brands, designers and celebrities. Georgie was always getting freebies and she was very creative with her style. I could hear her telling Suzie that she'd stitched on the flowers herself.

I once tried to sew a swimming badge on to my school blazer and somehow managed to sew the jumper I was wearing at the time to the blazer sleeve. I ripped the jumper and the blazer when I tried to detach myself.

Fashion is not my strong point.

"Well, who cares what Suzie Bravo

thinks?" Kizzy said sternly, as she swept her light brown hair back into a smooth ponytail. "Clara is lucky to have a sister like you to stand up for her. It was very brave of you to face those bullies. I wouldn't have been able to do it."

I smiled. This was, of course, a lie. Kizzy is the nicest person in the world and I would know because we've been best friends for ever. She lives on the same road as me and we've been "joined at the hip" (as my dad says) since our first day at school. We're both quite shy so it makes sense to just quietly stick together, while people like Suzie Bravo enjoy being the centre of attention.

But just because she's shy and petite – one of the shortest girls in our year, in fact – it doesn't mean Kizzy isn't brave enough to stand up to bullies. At the beginning of term, I accidentally kicked a football at Mr

Mercury, our grumpy new science teacher, and it bounced right off his big bald head. As he turned around slowly with this fierce expression on his face to see who the culprit was, Kizzy stepped forwards to apologize. I tried to protest but she told me very sternly to be quiet. And because she's the nicest person in the world, Mr Mercury just told her to be more careful in the future and that was that. He even laughed. That's the power Kizzy has over people. She can make the grumpiest science teacher on the planet laugh.

Later, she told me she took the blame because I'd already had a bad start with Mr Mercury. The week of the football incident, I had been shaking my pen to get it to work and accidentally flicked blue ink all over his crisp white shirt. She didn't want me to get into even more trouble.

If that's not bravery, I don't know what is.

As Mrs Damsel told us all to quieten down for the beginning of class, I tried to forget about my lame scar conversation and instead focus on the weirdness that had come shooting from my hands in the playground, and whether that was normal or not. I couldn't recall anyone else in our year spark lightning at their classmates, but maybe it was just part of growing up and I was ahead of everyone else. Mum did say recently that I was looking taller, so maybe it was growing pains or something?